MISS BUDGE GOES TO FOUNTAIN CITY

....

A MILDRED BUDGE
CHRISTMAS STORY

DAPHNE SIMPKINS

Quotidian Books

Daphne Simpkins/Quotidian Books
Montgomery, AL
www.DaphneSimpkins.org

Publisher's Note: This is a work of fiction. Names, characters, places, and incidents are a product of the author's imagination. Locales and public names are sometimes used for atmospheric purposes. Any resemblance to actual people, living or dead, or to businesses, companies, events, institutions, or locales is completely coincidental.

Miss Budge Goes to Fountain City/ Daphne Simpkins. -- 1st ed.
ISBN 978-1-7320158-3-8

Contents

For Ron and Sue Luckey
with gratitude for your friendship

Every day is a good day. Christmas, too.

–Mildred Budge

1

WHAT'S IN THE
MYSTERY BOX?

Mildred Budge had not always been a gambler.

But after she went into business with her friend Fran Applewhite, it had become partially her responsibility to restock their inventory over at their two antique booths in the local Emporium. When Mildred couldn't find anything to buy at the early morning estate sale, she had to choose something because she couldn't go home empty-handed.

So, the devout church lady gambled on a mystery box.

There was no instinct in her that prompted the purchase.

The moment didn't feel lucky.

God didn't tell her to buy it.

Mildred Budge bought the mystery box because it had a plastic handle on the top that felt like it would hold together long enough for her to carry to the car, and the box was priced at the amount of money she had in the side pocket of her purple corduroy pants: ten dollars.

"Here you go," Mildred said to the unshaven, sleepy college boy wearing a yellow T-shirt with the incongruous words on the front: Estate Sales R Us. The company specialized in helping relatives clean out the houses of the recently deceased, doing all the work for a nifty 30% of the gross receipts for the day.

After handing over her money, Mildred walked through the house toward the front door without pausing to examine any of the vintage keepsake holiday ornaments on the Christmas tree in the foyer. The ornaments were also for sale. Mildred caught a glimpse of Elvis Presley in a startling white outfit with bell bottom pants ostensibly having just sung "Blue Christmas," a duo of chipmunks wearing Santa hats waving silver icicles like swords, Betty Boop in a fur-lined red outfit blowing a kiss, and all kinds of reindeer in different sizes and prices that sparkled. Some reindeer were playful and Rudolphish. Other reindeer were stately and august. Mildred Budge had an affection for reindeer that she did not actively cultivate; but when she saw Prancer, the retired fifth grade school teacher smiled appreciatively. She adored Prancer!

But seeing Prancer was enough. Mildred Budge didn't need to own a reindeer ornament. She could enjoy seeing Prancer and walk right on by; so, she did, lugging the mystery box which had grown heavy fast.

Mildred walked back to her car, positioning the prize box in the back seat and stopping only briefly to inhale the sharp winter air. Somewhere nearby someone had a kitchen window cracked and was frying bacon for breakfast.

A door slammed loudly, and a woman called out, "Honey, come on inside. Breakfast's ready."

"She's the one frying bacon," Mildred whispered to God. "And I'm going home and make some for myself."

Mildred had eaten only one piece of toast with the last teaspoon of homemade pear preserves that one of her Sunday school chums had given her—it was barely enough to cover the toast! -- and she had sipped a fast cup of strong coffee. As a consequence of that meager repast, Mildred Budge was hungry.

Shoppers had to hit estate sales early if they were going to get the best bargains, and she had been up since 5 AM in order to get to it by 7:15, which was her arrival time. That fifteen minutes past the starting hour of the estate sale had cost her some of the best deals. The other vendors had gotten there at 6:30 and powered through, making fast decisions and handing

3

over their dollars with the kind of assurance Mildred did not feel when she made a purchase.

Still, she had bought something. Fran's business partner had snagged a mystery box.

And now with that well-taped cardboard box safely procured to fulfill her obligation to find some items to replenish their always dwindling inventory, Mildred was going home and cook a proper breakfast and then practice her Christmas carols on her old Baldwin studio piano for the Bereans, the members of her long-time Sunday school class. The girls expected her to get them in the holiday spirit by helping them sing the songs of the season.

'First, a proper breakfast and then I shall practice the carols so that my hands won't shake on Sunday morning,' Mildred resolved.

That was the plan.

2

AN ELF ON YOUR DOORSTEP

FOR CHRISTMAS

When Mildred reached her snug little bungalow in the garden district of Montgomery's old Cloverdale, someone was waiting for her: the loneliest woman Mildred had ever known.

Which was a paradox. For her visitor Dixie had multiple personality disorder. With all those voices inside of her to keep her company, Dixie was still very lonely.

Older than Mildred, Dixie sat splay-legged like a kid on Mildred's doorstep wearing a red and green elf costume. No hat! But Dixie had on a stretchy red and white striped shirt and a pair of green shorts that reached her knees. She was also wearing one of those Christmas light necklaces, and the small bulbs hanging around Dixie's neck were flashing green, red, blue, and yellow.

Mildred was not feeling nearly as festive. She was wearing her years-old purple corduroy pants suit that she kept folded and on a small white stool just inside her bedroom closet next to the sturdy low-heeled walking shoes she liked to wear outside of the house. Inside each pair of her outdoor shoes, Mildred kept the matching socks, the ones she wore for an hour at a time when running errands and then balled up and tucked back in the shoes. After three outings, she washed them out by hand in the bathroom sink and hung them over the shower rod to dry for a day or so until she could put them back in their proper place— into the pair of shoes to which they belonged.

On the floor in her closet were her dressier shoes for church: brown, black, and navy. In each pair of shoes was its matching dress socks. It was a system of order that Mildred needed now that she was becoming slightly color blind due, she believed, to the cataracts which had gotten demonstrably worse in the last year. She needed to get the silver cataract film that was distorting her vision removed, but she was waiting for the right time. It was hard for a church lady to find the right time to be incapacitated, because she was so very busy.

"Good morning, Dixie," Mildred called out after she had turned off the car and swung her legs through the open car door.

The other woman didn't speak at first. Maybe Dixie didn't hear the greeting. This silence did not alarm or confuse Mildred, for so many of her friends and acquaintances had hearing challenges. Moving slowly because of the cold, Mildred retrieved the mystery box from the back seat and then praying, "Jesus, walk with me," under her breath, she approached Dixie cautiously, wondering which personality was going to be present that morning.

You never knew which Dixie had come to visit. Mildred had never seen the elf costume before.

It seemed to fit Dixie pretty well. An angular, lanky woman in her sixties, Dixie often had the bearing and curiosity of a kid who couldn't sit still. Mildred had taught fifth graders for twenty-five years, and she knew a lot about restless kids. Dixie was one of them, just older. She had chosen Mildred Budge to be her friend.

Mildred was not surprised to see Dixie. She had taken to showing up at odd times, making herself at home and staying until some inner prompt signaled to her it was time to leave.

"Gone I am" is how Dixie often announced her leave-takings.

Mildred wanted to say the same words right then and just disappear. She often felt that way at Christmas. There was so much socializing to do, and it was more than Mildred's solitary temperament could handle. For Mildred Budge was a quiet person; and in her retirement from teaching, that aspect of her had grown even more appreciative of silence and stillness and something the world didn't know much about: peace. Even the Hallmark Christmas movies didn't celebrate peace and good will. It was more about romance and snow, cocoa and cookies, lost and found loves. Mildred had been lost a long time ago but found by One who had not left her an orphan even after the death of both parents. Mildred often enjoyed TV Christmas movies, but they almost never depicted the love-steeped season that she and her Berean sisters knew and relished. In Mildred's church lady world, Christmastime was Jesustime.

"Merry Christmas, Mildred Budge! Where have you been? I've been waiting hours. Thought you might have gone to see Santa Claus to give him your wish list. What do you want for Christmas?" Dixie demanded brightly, but before Mildred could marvel at being asked that question and wonder if she had any kind of an answer to it, Dixie asked another question. "Whatcha got there?"

Sometimes Dixie's greetings were a clue about which one of her personalities was present, and in that jovial hello, Mildred knew that the woman she had first met in a hospital waiting room was not the elf with her that morning. The version of Dixie waiting for her was a fourteen-year-old girl who liked to climb trees and snack incessantly.

Dixie took the door key out of Mildred's hand where her fingers were curled around it, unlocked Mildred's front door, and said, "Get on in the house, girl. It's cold out here, and my butt's frozen solid from sitting on that concrete step. You got anything to eat? I'm hungry."

Putting the box down heavily on the foyer floor, Mildred turned and faced her guest. "I've been to an estate sale."

The lights on Dixie's necklace flashed disconcertingly in the house, and the effect was like a loud noise. Covering her eyes, Mildred turned away from it and the kind of Christmas cheer it represented. Bright lights. Loud noise. And the pressure that others had expectations of her to enjoy and celebrate Christmas in a forced festive way. Mildred's festive side had receded over time. It had been replaced by perseverance and endurance. Patience, too.

"Why didn't you ask me to go? I love estate sales!" Dixie exclaimed, beginning a hurried rotation around the room, touching various items. Dixie often needed to touch household items in Mildred's house to make sure she was in the right place.

Today was no different.

9

Mildred waited while Dixie made her rounds of the foyer, the living room, and the kitchen where she looked for a snack while Mildred mulled over the best way to achieve peace in her own home. She didn't have a clue. Dixie did not obey the laws of polite society. She showed up early, barged in, stayed as long as she liked, and disappeared suddenly when she remembered something that needed her attention and which she had forgotten until that very moment. *Gone I am.*

Mildred prayed inwardly for Dixie to say the magic words "Gone I am" sooner rather than later. She was tired—and something else too: the church lady was braced for the holidays because they were hard. Being braced against the future took a toll on you.

"I want a bowl of Cheerios and a banana," Dixie announced, staring intently at Mildred.

"I don't have a banana," Mildred replied, moving toward the kitchen, where she put out two bowls and pointed to the box of Cheerios on top of the refrigerator where they dried out from being up so high near the air vent in the ceiling. Mildred knew this, but it was too late for her to change where she stored her boxes of cereal. Her parents had kept boxes of cereal on top of their refrigerator and a box of Kleenex, and that's where Mildred kept her cereal and tissues. She knew the location was not ideal, but she always instinctively now remembered where they were. Mildred felt that if she moved too much stuff from where it had always been, the new relocations, no matter how much more efficient and sensible, could cause some kind of internal disorientation in her memory from which she wouldn't easily recover. It was hard to change your ways. To budge. Mildred had been teased about her stolid habits all of her life.

As Dixie was standing by the kitchen sink spooning her Cheerios, dribbling milk down her chest unselfconsciously, she talked non-stop, ending with the questions that gave Mildred time to swallow: "What's in that box? When you gonna open that big old box? I'll help you. I'm very good at opening boxes. Don't you worry. If something live jumps out, I'll catch it and throw it out the back door. You know, like a racoon or a cat. Or, if it's the dismembered head of someone, I'll call the cops for you, and give you an alibi. You didn't walk in here with blood on your hands. Everyone knows you don't kill people and chop off their heads."

Then, Dixie eyed Mildred with a fresh curiosity, as if she weren't saying, 'You don't kill people, do you?'

"I hope it will be some items we can sell at our booths at the Emporium. I was shopping for inventory," Mildred replied, as she spooned the first bite of a child's portion of Cheerios. Five spoonsful later she placed her bowl with the rest of the sweet milk in the sink. Had she been alone the church lady would have slurped the remainder of the sweet milk from the bowl. Mildred did that all the time when she was watching the evening news alone and having cereal for supper. But Mrs. Budge's daughter did not slurp milk in front of other people. Southern women raised right, and who are all of their lives a testament to their good mother's home training, never slurp milk from a bowl in front of other people even in their own kitchen.

Mildred was just running some water in her cereal bowl, regretfully washing the rest of the sweet milk down the drain, when Dixie held her own bowl to her lips and gulped the remaining milk, wiping her lips on the back of her other hand afterwards and grinning. "That was good. But I'm still hungry. Cereal is more like an appetizer than a whole meal. Do you have anything else to eat?"

Mildred decided to distract Dixie from rummaging through her refrigerator or pantry by redirecting her to the living room. "We can open that big old mystery box now if you are still curious."

There was no hesitation.

Dixie hurried back to the living room, calling out over her shoulder, "I'm going to put the box on the side table so we can reach it. You better bring a knife or some scissors. There's a lot of tape on that box. And it looks like the bad kind of tape. You know that kind of tape that has little threads running through it so that you can't rip it with your hands? Your box has that kind of tape."

When Mildred joined her, Dixie leaned over the box and listened with great concentration, looking up at Mildred with rainbow eyes reflecting the colors of her blinking necklace, to say reassuringly, "I don't hear anything ticking."

3

HOW DO YOU OPEN A MYSTERY BOX?

Dixie opened the pair of scissors Mildred had brought from the kitchen junk drawer, and holding the blades exposed, she used one extended blade tip pointed down and finger braced against its side to rip through the bad kind of tan tape affixed to the top of the box.

There were no wasted motions, and Mildred marveled at that. She struggled to open well-taped boxes, tightly sealed envelopes, and vacuum-packed jars.

She didn't say that, however. Instead, Mildred asked, "Aren't you cold?"

"A little bit," Dixie boasted. "I like being a little cold. It's one of the ways I lose weight."

"What?"

"Yeah. You know how much I love to eat?"

"I do," Mildred confirmed, already trying to figure out what she was going to make the two of them for lunch because it was obvious that Dixie had no immediate plans to say 'Gone I am.'

"Well, if I get any fatter, I won't fit into my clothes. I don't want to have to buy a new wardrobe because I don't have any money, so I try to stay a little cold. Your body has to burn more calories to keep you warm. It amazes me that more people don't do that."

"Where did you learn that?" Mildred asked, privately wondering if Dixie's facts were true. *Would that work? She needed to lose a pound or two herself.* But she hated being cold. All the Bereans hated being cold.

"I didn't learn it anywhere. I thought it out all by my lonesome." Dixie waited to see if Mildred got her joke. She had been saving that joke for just the right moment. If anyone was ever not all by her lonesome, it was somebody with multiple personalities.

Mildred nodded. And when she nodded, Mildred saw a loose Cheerio stuck to her left bosom where it had been rising and falling with each breath. Any other friend but Dixie would have told Mildred Budge that she had a Cheerio stuck on her chest, but Dixie was fully engaged in opening the box.

"You burn calories to lose weight. If you're cold, you have to burn more of your own calories to get warm. As soon as the days start getting cold, I try to go around a little underdressed. It's my diet trick, especially during the holidays when there is so much food to eat. Look here," she said, folding back the cardboard flaps. "You've got yourself a couple of lime green Frisbees."

"I was afraid of that," Mildred said, plucking the Cheerio off and popping it in her mouth. She swallowed it, wondering if she just stopped eating the crumbs and leftovers that landed on her bosom would she lose weight? *Was that a viable diet trick?*

"You've got yourself two fine Frisbees," Dixie announced, ripping the flaps of the box all the way open. "Really good ones. They have been around the block a few times, but you would expect that, wouldn't you? How else would you know if they worked?"

"Indeed," Mildred replied. The two Frisbees were battered and scarred with bruises, dents, and dirt. Someone wearing a yellow T-shirt with the words Estate Sales R Us could have fished those two green Frisbees out of a random trash bin and stuffed them in a mystery box in order to charge ten dollars for them. Any woman who has taught public school and lived long enough to be managing on a fixed income could easily imagine that to be true.

"You don't want them?" Dixie confirmed.

Mildred shook her head gently. "I'm not a Frisbee thrower," she replied truthfully.

Dixie laid them on top of the clean tablecloth and said with admiration, "Don't you just love the color though, especially this time of year? I love green," Dixie said, patting her knee-length shorts, which were a Kelly green.

"Do you think you ought to turn off your necklace while you're inside? It's wasting the battery life"

"Oh, no," Dixie said. "You're never wasting a battery if you're lighting up the world. That's how I see it, anyway."

"All right then," Mildred said, pointing to the box. There was more inside. A layer of crumpled newspaper pages separated the packed items. Only one newspaper page had been used to cover the Frisbees. Dixie had tossed it unceremoniously to the floor.

"You want a go at it?" Dixie offered, kicking at the wad of paper at her feet.

Dixie was having such a good time Mildred exhaled and shook her head. "Go ahead. You're doing fine."

"I love surprises," Dixie said, yanking out more wadded up newspaper pages. "You've got yourself some stuffed animals," she announced, holding up the first one, an indistinguishable critter.

It might have been white once upon a time. Now, it was greyish, and it smelled of damp cat. *Yes, a wet cat.* One sniff was enough. Mildred didn't want to name it more specifically.

"Poor thing isn't exactly pretty, is it?"   Mildred asked, tactfully. The boy in the yellow T-shirt could easily have fished out these ugly, dirty stuffed animals from the same trash bin where he had found the Frisbees. She felt grieved in her spirit for him. People like that walked the earth. Yes, they did. Her soul hurt with the knowledge.

"I can't even tell what it is," Dixie said, scrunching up her face. "But I know where it came from. This is one of those critters you win in those mall arcade games with the big silver metal claw. Costs you fifty cents to try. And sometimes you just have to try. But when you win, you don't. They look like this. Critters of unknown origin. I think they are supposed to be monsters from an underworld where evil lives and tries to come up through the ground and grab the ankles of children walking overhead. I think that's what those monsters do. I don't know what monsters are doing in a Christmas box," Dixie said with scorn.

She brought out two more dirty monsters, her expression darkening. "Mildred Budge, you've been ripped off is what has happened here today. They were probably blue, yellow, and white when they were first shipped here from Taiwan or China. But now they are the color of a dirty sky, a dirty daisy, and dirty

19

snow. These critters are mocking the planet earth. At the very least, they are not very Christmasy. Not even a little bit. How much did you spend on this box?" she demanded to know suddenly.

The answer stuck in Mildred's throat.

Dixie waited.

Finally, Mildred admitted: "Ten dollars. And no, they're not very Christmasy," Mildred agreed, reaching for them. "Or valuable."

"What are you going to do with them?"

"Throw them away," Mildred replied readily.

Her answer startled Dixie, who thought about the reply, and then out of a sober respect for Mildred's loss of ten dollars and the disappointment in the contents of the mystery box, Dixie turned off her blinking necklace.

"I guess that's all you can do with them. You can't give them to a child. They're too dirty, and you certainly can't sell them at the Emporium."

"They are," Mildred replied, glad that Dixie was being reasonable.

"You gonna throw away the Frisbees?" Dixie demanded.

"I haven't thought about the Frisbees," Mildred said, her attention flitting to the clock on the wall, her empty stomach, her tired feet, her craving for silence, and her calendar upon which she had scheduled her Christmas to-do list.

Dixie picked up the Frisbees again, holding them in her hand and grinning. "Don't you just love this color?"

Before Mildred could reply, Dixie demanded, "You go next."

Discouraged but persevering, Mildred made her hands go under the next layer of newspaper, reaching into the dark bottom of the mystery box where she felt around for what was left. She found something solid. Heavy. Something wooden. With points. Sharp edges, too.

"What is it?" Dixie asked, leaning in and peering, her body intruding upon Mildred's personal space.

Mildred tried not to back away or turn her head, for Dixie interpreted such moves of adjustment as personal offense and long-lasting rejection. So, Mildred held her crouching-over-the-box position, offered a benign church lady smile, and lifted out a vintage music box bedecked with a tall slender Christmas tree in the middle and a circle of angels poised to fly around it when the music played.

In spite of herself, Mildred smiled. It was something—this music box.

Dixie's eyes widened and began to glow. She clapped her hands softly, the way veteran cheerleaders do as they age, forgetting over time that they are not wearing striped twirling skirts in their school colors and holding red and white pom poms. Cheerleaders keep this soft, hand clapping response, and this was a rare moment when Mildred Budge understood the impulse of that instinctive cheer. Mildred agreed. *Yes, this music box deserves applause.*

For Mildred could see right away that the music box had been crafted by someone who understood quality, symmetry, and beauty. When she looked at the color of blue around its base and the thick gold turntable upon which the tree and angels would rotate, she thought that the burnished golden sheen of the turntable was lovely, matching the scattering of gold stars that encircled the sky-blue base.

Mildred held the music box up to the light coming in from the window. The faces of the angels were distinct, wearing not the expressions of holiness one would expect, but of mischief. "The angels are little rascals. Scamps," Mildred whispered approvingly. She had always hoped that there were some mischievous angels somewhere. True or not, she now knew there was at least someone else in the world who hoped similarly. The artist who had painted the faces on the angels had also hoped that some angels somewhere were not just delivering messages of death and doom but were having fun going here and there.

For just a moment—a fraction of time, really—Mildred Budge felt less alone in the world because of the artist who had painted the angels' expressions just so.

A short-bodied brass key jutted out on the side, daring the new owner to turn it. Mildred's thumb and forefinger did that without her permission. And when she pressed gently on the key, Mildred heard a tiny squeak—a single sharp note. No more.

But that single sound was something. It was a beginning. An echoing ping of hope!

There was the possibility of music to come. When she realized that, Mildred Budge's brown eyes began to glow like Dixie's, and if you looked closely, like the mischievous angels' too.

4

THE WINTER LIGHT CAN BE BLINDING

"Can I have the Frisbees?" Dixie asked, suddenly.

Mildred nodded dismissively, as the other woman forgot that she was too old to want a Frisbee.

Turning abruptly, Dixie walked to the back door exiting the sun porch. There, holding the first lime green Frisbee like it was an Olympic disc, Dixie threw it as hard as she could out into the field that connected Mildred's house to her neighbors, Sam and Belle Deerborn. Then, she watched the first spinning green disc sail and fall.

Just that quick, she sent the second Frisbee flying. It, too, fell. "I hate that. I wanted them to land high up in a tree, but they both fell right onto the ground. They're just going to lay there doing nothing."

"Why did you want them to land in the tree?" Mildred asked, her grip tightening on the music box. She was beginning to tremble slightly from the cold air that came in when the back door opened and because she was hungry.

Mildred walked over and looked out in her back field, wondering if Sam and Belle would mind the two green Frisbees decorating their yard until she could trek out later into the field after Dixie was gone, retrieve them, and place them securely in the garbage can.

Dixie shrugged playfully. "Just so we would have something to watch during the next rain storm. Imagine watching the rain late some afternoon when it's even colder than it is today and waiting for those two green Frisbees to fall out of a tree and each of us making a wish. That would be excitement right there. Pure excitement. Not to mention two free wishes. We could make smores on the stove and pretend we are camping out."

Before Mildred could try to explain that a Frisbee falling from a tree was not the same event as a star falling that you wished upon, Dixie said. "You gonna turn that key on the music box?"

Mildred had already surreptitiously tried the brass key with a bit more pressure, but it was stuck. Really stuck. Mildred didn't want to force the key, and she didn't want rambunctious Dixie to break the music box even more than it probably already was. Like a doctor who knows the coming dire diagnosis but doesn't deliver it right away to family members bent on believing in a miracle, Mildred Budge postponed telling Dixie that the music box was broken.   Still, believing that projected outcome to be true, Mildred didn't want either one of them to break the music box more. Time would have to pass. Prayers would need to be uttered. The music box would need to be dusted, wiped down, and set on a table in the morning's light and keep her company before Mildred Budge would give up on it having some kind of redemptive value, if only to look good on the table for a while until she couldn't bear having something useless cluttering up her house any longer, for goodness' sake.

The verdict would keep until she finally gave up and said, with regret, because it is always hard for someone to witness another's experience of reality: "The music box is broken. But the angels are cute. And that tree in the middle is elegant. Simply elegant."

"I wonder what its song will be when we get it to working," Dixie mused, confident that a happy ending for the music box was imminent. "Probably "Silent Night." They usually play that song," Dixie said.

"They do," Mildred agreed. Although it had been a long time since she had heard a music box play any song. Even the glass-domed music box with an angel encased inside playing a horn that she kept stored safely in her china cabinet and brought out on Christmas Eve was rarely turned on. Mildred mostly looked at it. Dusted it about every other month. She could tell others that it played "O Holy Night," but Mildred couldn't recall a recent Christmas when she had turned the brass key of that glass music box and listened to that carol. No, it had been a long time. Years.

"It's dirty, isn't it? You want me to run some water on it?" Dixie asked, leaning forward. "I could put this band of angels in the sink and give them a good bath." When Dixie moved toward the music box, her body blocked the light, and Mildred was momentarily blinded.

It was her cataracts. With a change in light or when someone blocked the light from falling exactly right where her eyes were focused, Mildred's clarity of vision became obscured. Too much light and the world had a silver screen across it. Not enough light and Mildred couldn't see shapes, true depth, distinguish dark colors, or focus easily on the notes of music on the page of the hymnal.

"It's so dusty," Dixie said, leaning forward and blowing across the surface of the burnished gold turntable.

Specs of dust flew up and into Mildred's eyes. Startled, Mildred tried to blink the dust away, but that didn't work.

With the sudden panic that occurs when you have soap or dirt in your eyes, Mildred resisted rubbing her eyes for that would only make the burning in her eyes worse. Instead, she said in the tradition of church ladies who automatically apologize for others' mistakes, "Excuse me. I'll be back in a minute."

Mildred turned away from the music box and, blinking rapidly, hurriedly made the short walk to the bathroom where she flushed her eyes with cupped cold water and then rinsed off her sturdy brown plastic glasses that were speckled with the angels' dust. Blotting her face, Mildred stared at her reflection in the mirror over the sink. "You look tired, and Christmas is coming. You're going to get a lot more tired before it's over. You better get a grip on yourself. Buck up."

She had a long Christmas list of work to do-- dishes to cook, cards to write, and those carols to practice, practice, practice on the piano so that she could play on Sunday mornings when the Bereans sang their way through the traditional Christmas carols: "O Little Town of Bethlehem," "Joy to the World," "Oh Come All Ye Faithful," and she needed at least one more. It wouldn't be "O Holy Night" though because the range of that song was too expansive for any woman in the Berean class. That inspiring anthem of Christmas was reserved for younger, stronger soloists who could manage a two-octave range. They could also sing "A Mighty Fortress." The Bereans never sang "A Mighty Fortress" either.

'I'm going to need at least one more carol,' Mildred thought. A carol a week between Thanksgiving and Christmas. She would have to find it, practice it, and remind herself to play it in a steady, even rhythm that the other ladies could follow. The Bereans loved to sing; but they had soft voices, unreliable hearing, and, well, they weren't accustomed to making much noise because they attended an old-fashioned church where the women moved and lived in quiet submission to men who were in charge of making plans, managing the money, paying the bills, and protecting them from the Evil One.

Turning away from the sight of her own face in the mirror, Mildred Budge walked with resolve back down the hallway to the kitchen where Dixie was still waiting for her. Her legs felt wooden. She was older than she had ever been in her life. But when Mildred saw Dixie, she smiled because church ladies smile no matter how tired they are, how hungry, or how old they feel.

"You picked a funny time to wash your face," Dixie said, running her hands over the small carved angels on top of the music box.

Oblivious to Mildred's discomfort with the dust from the box and the fatigue of disciplined good will, Dixie leaned forward, peered intently at the music box and asked, "Why are angels so often naked?"

5

WHY ARE ANGELS
SO OFTEN NAKED?

Mildred leaned closer, ignoring the question about the naked angels though she took note of it. *Why are angels so often naked*? "This music box is German made. And the gold...well, it could be some kind of gold leaf. Something like that." It wasn't shiny. It gleamed. If her best friend and business partner Fran had been with them, she would have known what that gold finish was.

"There are five fat angels, and not one of them has a stitch of clothes on. Look at their little low-hanging fat bellies. I like fat-bellied angels." Dixie patted her own belly companionably. "Have you noticed that the older you get the harder it is to hold in your stomach? I gave up a while back and was kind of relieved to stop caring what my stomach does when left to its own devices. I don't even try to manage it anymore." And then without taking a breath, Dixie counted the angels' instruments. "One trumpet. One flute. One harp. You'd think there'd be more harps. And then a drum. That fifth angel must have been holding a trumpet, but he's empty-handed now. Looks like he's blowing a kiss, and that's okay with me. Or maybe he's whistling. He's holding his mouth funny. Yep. That angel could be whistling Jesus. Do angels whistle while they work? This angel looks like he could. Why couldn't somebody put some pants on an angel?"

Before Mildred could count the angels and their instruments for herself, Dixie asked, "Why do you suppose someone put a music box this nice in a box with all that other crap?"

That question was easier to answer than the one about the angels being naked.

It was time to say the words out loud. Like other church ladies, Mildred chose her moments to say anything. Dixie was different. Ideas and questions tumbled out of her mouth uncensored, unfiltered, and she didn't try to hold her stomach in anymore. Mildred took note of that idea. She had been thinking about buying some special underpants that helped to hold in your stomach, but she was afraid the elastic around the pants would cause a rash. Mildred feared rashes.

Unavoidably, the moment arrived, and Mildred told the truth. "Because the music box is broken.

34

That's why it's in there with the other things. The music box looks good, but it doesn't work. It won't play a song," Mildred predicted. "It probably never will."

To prove her point, Mildred used her thumb and forefinger on her left hand to grip and turn with greater resolve the tarnished brass key on the side of the music box one more truth-telling time. Nothing happened. Not even a single resounding note occurred this time.

In spite of her good sense, Mildred Budge was disappointed, because deep inside, when mature church ladies expect the worst, they still hope for the best. *The music box really is broken*, she thought, *Oh, it is so pretty too*. Mildred looked more closely at the small gold stars hand painted around the base. Very delicate work. The star points were sharp and distinct, with a thin line of black outlining them, causing them to stand out against the blue. The varnish was rich, a thick protective shine. Mildred was approving of the quality of varnish applied over the paint when she realized that the dust on the music box was gone and that Dixie had cleaned the music box without supervision. Mildred experienced a moment's alarm when she wondered if Dixie had rinsed off the wooden box with metal parts inside under the sink's faucet, but then she spied the mound of soiled paper towels that looked damp with dirt. *Dixie had used those. Okay. Okay. Dixie could be left alone and not destroy the house or the things in it.*

"It cost somebody a pretty penny once upon a time," Dixie said, settling back. "I'd like to see the angels fly. I wonder what song it will play," Dixie said, her faith unshaken that one day it would. "We used to have an ice cream truck that went through the neighborhood playing 'Take me out to the ballgame.'" She sniffed the air suddenly, hungrily. "What do I smell?" Dixie asked suddenly. "Do you smell what I smell?"

Dixie had not closed the back-door tightly, and that small crack was letting in the chilly air.

"Tea olive," Mildred said, taking a deep breath.

Leaving the beautiful but silent music box on the table, the retired school teacher walked over to the back door, preparing to close it, and hesitated. She kept Dixie company instead while the other woman, lost in thought, stared outside at the two dormant Frisbees on the ground, the shadowy lights of Sam's and Belle's lonely house, and the way the wintry morning light played on the trees.

What was the experience of time for her? Mildred wondered. She often wondered that about everyone she was with sooner or later. Really. *What was life like for her? For him?*

That wasn't the only kind of question asked about Dixie, however.

Other people asked Mildred Budge heartbreaking questions about Dixie. "What do you suppose happened to her to make her personality split up into lots of little selves, bless her heart?"

The answers to questions asked about Dixie were the kind you pieced together for yourself after watching television cop shows. Something really bad must have happened to Dixie as a little girl to cause her to produce a dozen or more people who lived inside of her, each of them taking a turn hiding out from strangers. Except Mildred. Dixie was loose and free with her selves with Mildred Budge.

"The music box doesn't have to stay broken," Dixie announced suddenly. "Those angels could fly if we could get the music going again," Dixie replied, and her face broke into a big smile just as the sun came from behind a cloud and lit up the room.

Mildred raised the music box over her head and read a name engraved in a gold cursive writing on the bottom. '*Was it Steinbach?*' Mildred squinted. Any other person in the room would have interpreted that squint as a cry for help—*You can't make out the letters! Are those cataracts bothering you again*? *Let me read that for you*.

But not Dixie.

37

"The immediate problem that I can see is that there is no one here in Montgomery, Alabama who is trained in repairing German music boxes," Mildred said.

"You say German as if that is especially good," Dixie said, suddenly performing a pirouette. She did three more rotations before coming to a stop. Then she turned to Mildred for the answer to her implied question.

"It is good," Mildred replied without explanation. *But was that true?* Did she just have a bias that assumed products were better made in Germany than by the hands of people in other countries? Did the Swiss make the best watches and chocolate? Did the Japanese have the tastiest drinkable aloe water? Did the British serve the best tea? Did Southerners make the best fried chicken?

"Would the repairman have to be German?" Dixie asked, her expression growing pensive.

"No," Mildred answered. "He—or she-- just needs to be able to fix things and…. respect beauty."

Dixie snapped the fingers on her right hand; and with that motion, her necklace started blinking again. Delighted, Dixie boasted, "I think I know someone who can fix that music box."

Mildred looked up, not expecting to have an answer to her question arrive so quickly—no praying, no seeking, no opening of the Bible, no fasting. No price of time and attention to pay for the gift of a solution.

"Are you telling me that one of your hidden, shyer personalities can fix music boxes?" Mildred asked cautiously. It was not an easy question to ask.

"Maybe," Dixie said, pausing as if considering that idea. "But I don't think so," Dixie said, placing a hand on the music box as if she were a nurse taking the pulse of a real live human being. "I have heard about a man over in Fountain City who can fix anything."

"Fountain City?" Mildred repeated, brow wrinkling. Fountain City was over the river and through the woods. Well, not woods, exactly. But Fountain City's Main Street was a good twenty miles or so from where she lived in Old Cloverdale, two miles from downtown Montgomery. The round trip? Forty miles, give or take.

It had been years since Mildred Budge had driven the old route to Fountain City. She had stopped visiting Fountain City after her mother died. Her mother had liked to go that way and visit her kinfolk during the holidays. Her brother Tommy used to drive them because Mildred's dad worked during the weekdays, and Tommy had flexibility in his schedule to drive his sister and niece around.

"Let's run over there right now and see if we can make some fat angels fly," Dixie proposed.

"Right now?" Mildred asked, jarred.

Spontaneity was not Mildred Budge's modus operandi. "What's the name of this business? What is this Mr. Fixit's legal name?"

Dixie shrugged. "I don't know. I just know that some guy who knows how to fix things has a Mr. Fixit shop in Fountain City on Main Street next door to a pie shop run by a lady who used to make fudge but now she makes pies. We could eat some pie while we are waiting on the music box to be fixed. I'm hungry. Those Cheerios weren't enough to keep me going."

It was a done deal in Dixie's mind. A no-brainer.

There was a man who could fix things. She knew where he was. And there was pie to be eaten next door. They could eat pie and get the music box fixed. In Dixie's world that kind of thinking happened easily and optimistically.

Mildred thought otherwise. If Mr. Fixit existed, they would have to leave the music box which would mean a return visit, get a receipt and not lose it, and obtain an estimate before agreeing to pay a bill, and who knows how much he would charge? Mildred was already out ten bucks. And the pie served next door would be ordinary. It was a rare occasion now when a piece of pie served anywhere wasn't some thawed-out- previously-frozen slice of tasteless dough with an imitation fruity filling that tasted sweet but nothing more. No inspirations of delicately measured spices had been added that would make a peach pie peachier, a strawberry pie strawberrier, a pear pie pearier.

As if reading her mind, Dixie said, "Her pies are sublime. That's what they say. I've heard that word used just like that. That may be the name of her shop. Sublime Pies. I can't quite recall it. Grab your stuff, girlfriend, and let's make tracks."

Mildred could think of a dozen reasons not to make tracks to Fountain City at a little after ten in the morning. How did either of them know this Mr. Fixit would be there anyway?

Perhaps this Mr. Fixit went on vacation during the holiday season. How do you find out if a shop is open if you don't know the name of the shop?

Dixie read Mildred's reluctance to gamble on a trip to Fountain City.

"Don't you ever just want to run away from home?" Dixie asked. "I mean, it's nice here, but don't you ever want to see if the grass is greener somewhere else--have a piece of pie for lunch instead of a fried bologna sandwich?"

Mildred had never considered the idea. Not once. She loved being home. Loved her routine. Loved a fried bologna sandwich when the bread was fresh. And now that Dixie had mentioned it, *yes, yes,* a fried bologna sandwich sounded just right on her good fresh bread.

When Mildred didn't answer, Dixie asked another question.

"Don't you ever want to run away from your to-do list?"

No. Mildred loved her to-do list. Sometimes the chores or the idea of the chores made her tired. But Mildred Budge liked to work. She liked to plan.

Sensing that Mildred wasn't convinced, Dixie tried one more time.

"Don't you ever want to run away from Christmas?"

Mildred's answer was immediate and truthful.

"Yes. Yes, I have in years past and this year too wanted to run away from Christmas. Yes," Mildred said with conviction.

She couldn't stop saying yes, though the very idea that a good church lady would want to run away from the occasion during the year that marked the birth of Jesus, the reason for the season for a tried and true church lady of the South, was almost beyond explanation.

"Then, let's go. Let's go get some pie. You drive. I'll carry the music box in my lap."

"It will take the better part of this whole day," Mildred argued weakly.

"So?" Dixie asked, and when she said that one word, Dixie looked just like that angel whistling Jesus, and Mildred laughed.

"So…." Mildred said, stalling as she walked to the back door and tested the knob. She made sure the lock was turned.

It was a beautiful wintry day--brisk but not too cold. The November light was pretty on the trees. Out in the field two green Frisbees glinted in the fallen leaves, and Mildred smiled. It was as if children had been playing in her yard and left them behind—a promise of sorts that they would be back. Children. She missed children at Christmas. *Once a teacher always a teacher who loves children*….

And what a fool's task: to go on a pilgrimage to find a man who might not exist and whose name they didn't know but, if he was there and could fix things, might be able to repair a broken music box while she and Dixie ate an over-priced slice of pie. Now that Mildred thought about it, the pie would cost more than two dollars a slice, which is the maximum any piece of pie should ever cost in any restaurant. Any pie that is described by its maker as sublime would cost the mad money Mildred kept back in her wallet for special emergencies. Mildred Budge had passed a bakery three weeks ago that specialized in cupcakes, and those cupcakes cost three dollars each. A slice of sublime pie would cost no less, surely.

The proposed trip was an extravagant use of time. Mildred had an extensive list of work that must be done, and she could quote many verses in the Bible about doing your work. There was so much to do. Christmas was coming. The list of chores began to repeat in her mind: She needed to rehearse the Christmas carols for Sunday. The Berean Sunday school class liked to sing, and she had to practice those carols. And her eyesight wasn't trustworthy. She couldn't see the notes on the music so well right now. She needed to go to the eye doctor, and she didn't want to go to the eye doctor.

And then something like a Christmas miracle happened to Mildred Budge. She turned and saw all of the children who lived in Dixie, and they wanted an old-fashioned field trip.

Mildred looked into the eyes of Dixie, a woman with many personalities and said, "Yes. Let's go find Mr. Fixit."

6

WANT TO RUN AWAY FROM CHRISTMAS?

"Let's not talk about Jesus on the way," Dixie said, looking out the window.

She had changed just that fast. Sitting in the passenger seat of Mildred's car, Dixie was suddenly passive. Gone was the excited girl in an elf outfit who wanted to make fat angels fly. That Dixie had been replaced by another version of herself who was pensively staring out the window watching the scenes of Montgomery fly by. Yards and houses bore the recent decorations of orange and gold but were being replaced here and there with inflatable snowmen and Grinches accessorized with the colors red and green.

Mildred wondered how red and green had become the Christmas colors. She had a vague recollection about the picturesque images associated with Currier & Ives coming into accepted cultural prominence as a form of house art, but she didn't know about the colors.

Dixie was inside herself now, not wanting to hear about Jesus. Mildred heard the statement of fear and self-defense and resolved to pray on it later. For outside of Mildred Budge there was a paper to-do list, and inside of Mildred Budge there was this other cataloguing of moments in time that required thought and committed focused prayer. The prayer began in that moment, but the prayer was already alive in the future too, and in that way, Mildred traveled through time—was part of eternity though she didn't call it that.

In the present moment, Mildred's hands were firmly on the steering wheel, and Dixie's hands were firmly on the music box placed for safekeeping on her lap.

"What did you say?" Mildred asked quietly, just making sure that she had heard the other woman correctly.

"I'm not in the mood for Jesus today."

"You're not in the mood for Jesus?" Mildred asked, her voice neutral as she took the first gentle left curve that would lead to the river bridge. Repeating the idea was a church lady's stalling technique when she didn't know what to say, and Mildred didn't know what to say.

She was also concentrating on the road, for traffic had increased all of a sudden. There was a big truck

46

behind her driving too close, pressing her to go faster. The speed of most traffic was often too fast for Mildred. Her preference for a slower pace was not a part of being older with an older car either. Traffic had always been too fast for Mildred Budge. Slow was Mildred Budge's preferred speed for all activities. Even when reading a surprising romance about a church elder sweet-talking a proper church lady into holy matrimony, she had turned the pages of *LOVEJOY* slowly.

One of the deepest secrets of her life happened when as a young woman Mildred Budge had been pulled over by the police for driving too slowly. She had not been able to understand how there could be a law against going too slowly, but the policeman had pulled her over with his flashing blue lights, and rudely explained what she had been doing wrong, "You shouldn't drive with your foot on the brake. I followed you for a while and you keep tapping the brake. It will wear out your brakes, and the drivers behind you get nervous because no one knows what you are about to do."

Embarrassed and confused, the youthful Millie Budge had stared straight ahead while she thought he was writing out a ticket, but the policeman hadn't given her one, just the warning. *Don't ride with your foot on the brake.* And he had implanted the idea that the speed with which she preferred to live was slow to the point of being illegal; and in that way, this moseying daughter of the South was simply, by instinct and preference, assigned a judgment: she was wrong.

Mildred was not of the world that liked to zoom. That's the speed that the policeman used when he took off on his motorcycle, with a contemptuous dismissive parting wave of his left hand as if he knew she was watching him. She did, for Mr. Budge's daughter could not go back out in traffic right away. Millie cried some first because the policeman had scared her; and then flicking her left blinker on, she had looked carefully behind her and eased back out in the right lane that was clearly designated for drivers like her: *Slow drivers keep right.* Many street signs had those words on them.

Old Montgomery Highway had the tempo Mildred preferred, and the landscape was nostalgic, familiar, comforting. Or, it would be as soon as the bullying truck tailgating her gave up trying to make her go faster and passed her. She tried not to make eye contact with him in her rear-view mirror, letting her mind wander back in time to when she and her mother and Uncle Tommy made this drive during the holidays to visit their mother.

Years ago, so many years ago, there had been a business on the left side of the road that sold children's backyard playhouses. Long ago, there had been a model for a log cabin and another of a princess' castle playhouse. Ostensibly, doting parents had stopped and placed orders to have a playhouse like either of the models on display delivered to their home for their little girl or boy. Mildred had been a young girl in the backseat peering out of the window when she had seen the princess castle and been mystified that other little girls would want to play in it. Millie dreamed of a playhouse carved into the base of a big tree from which she would run a neighborhood library. There, she could loan her Nancy Drew and Hardy Boys books to her friends. Her reverie was interrupted by Dixie's sudden confession.

"I know I'm not supposed to say I'm not in the mood for Jesus, but really, it gets tiring sometimes trying to think Jesus up," Dixie said as the truck that had been traveling too fast veered out and passed them with a great harrumph, the kind of loud sound a man makes who stands up after a long sit at the dining table, and too much food later, groans his way to his feet. The truck chugged and moved on.

Instinctively, Mildred's foot eased up on the gas to give the truck driver more space between them. *Go on. No one's chasing you. You win. I am happy to lose.*

"Jesus is the reason for the season, and Jesus is the reason so many people chase their own tails in the name of righteousness," Dixie said, talking about Jesus when she had just told Mildred she didn't want to talk about him.

"Is that what you believe we're doing?" Mildred asked softly, as suddenly her Uncle Tommy forged up in her spirit, big and looming, like a battleship that appears suddenly on the horizon when the other smaller ships are in danger. She missed her Uncle Tommy as much as she missed anyone who had passed on to Glory. She wanted to say his name out loud just to hear it spoken—for old time's sake, whatever that meant. Christmas and the sudden sighting of the Alabama River made Mildred nostalgic. *Jesus,* she thought. *Jesus.* Inside his name was life itself: all time, all space, the past and the future all in one name. Everyone who said his name in hope—he didn't cast anyone away—abided forever inside his shepherd's embrace.

"What are you thinking about?" Dixie asked suddenly.

The truck. The river. Jesus. Uncle Tommy.

"My Uncle Tommy," Mildred said. "He used to drive mother and me this way to see his mother. My grandmother."

"It must be nice to have had an Uncle Tommy and a grandmother. And a mother," Dixie said, and her voice was small, her face turned toward the passenger window. She was deep inside herself, too.

Mildred's Uncle Tommy had been stalwart, steady, unflagging and had often driven her and her mother over the river to Fountain City to make the rounds of visiting the branch of her mother's family that lived out in the rural county across the river. Mildred could count how many family members had passed on and knew exactly how many were left; but in her mind, on a certain day when Uncle Tommy appeared on the horizon of her inner sea, everyone was still in place. Now, their hearts and minds and souls were pulsing with the beauty and truth of eternal life—and always would. *Jesus. Jesus.*

Although Dixie said she didn't want to talk about Jesus, she had more to say.

"I like the notion of Jesus all right, but I get worn out with all the ways you—not just you, everybody— says we have to pay our respects to him. Where two or more people are gathered in his name that's where he is. But I've been in all kinds of situations where two or more people sitting around together are saying his name, and I never saw Jesus.

"You'd think at least one of me would have seen Jesus by now, but none of us has. People think I'm crazy, but I never see Jesus, and people all around me with no one telling them that they've got too many people living inside of them talk like he's right in the room or the car.

"I don't ever call them crazy, but they feel pretty comfortable telling me something's wrong with me. And if they don't tell me, they think it. I can see that, but I don't see Jesus. And I don't go out of my way to call them crazy or even ask what terrible thing happened to them to make them crazy," Dixie said in a wounded tone of voice that was reporting pain rather than accusing others of guilt.

'But our sweet friend Dixie who keeps visiting our church and sharing suppers during fellowship nights has heard the questions,' Mildred thought. 'And she hasn't joined our church.'

Dixie had heard the questions they had asked. Were they asked to understand and sympathize with her condition or because their prurient curiosities couldn't be satisfied by their own troubles? So often the explanation was the latter: people often didn't ask certain questions out of love or concern. They asked out of a kind of morbid curiosity.

Dixie looked sideways at Mildred before confessing, "Sometimes I think people who see Jesus are the crazy people, and I'm, well…." She faltered. "You wouldn't say that to my face. You never say anything mean to anyone. Do you ever think mean thoughts?"

"Yes," Mildred said, her eyes on the road. "I think mean thoughts, and there have been times when I have said curse words. They flew right out of my mouth; and sometimes that happened right after I was praying, and I wondered right out loud to Jesus…. 'How can I sing a hymn and the next second or two another part of who I am says a curse word like that?'"

"Exactly!" Dixie said. "That's what it's like. I hear some of the things one of us says, and I wonder, 'Where'd that come from?' What's your favorite hymn? No. Not hymn. Christmas carol."

It was a sudden jarring switch in topic, but Mildred was used to that with Dixie. She leapfrogged. Zigged and zagged. Hop-scotched.

"It varies, depending on the day, my mood, and who is close enough to sing along with."

"Do you ever just answer a question plain, or do you always have to answer like a lawyer—like that. Like the way you just answered." Dixie's voice grew loud and irritable. "I asked you a simple question, and you won't answer it."

"Have Yourself a Merry Little Christmas," Mildred stated flatly. It would do for an answer in the moment.

"That's not a Christmas carol. That's not even a hymn. That's a song from a movie. I heard that song in a movie."

"A man from Alabama wrote it. I like the song, and that answer will do for today. I can change my mind tomorrow if someone asks me the same question."

Dixie stared out the window as they approached the bridge that would take them over the Alabama River. The sunlight was pretty on the cold choppy water. The Harriett II riverboat was parked right up close to the shore next to the part of downtown Montgomery where things were happening. Somebody in charge of the city was a mover and a shaker.

"Have you ever taken a ride on that boat?" Dixie asked suddenly. She was full of questions, but they were honest questions, not busybody questions, and not the kind of questions people used to defend themselves or delay answering until they thought of the right thing to say.

Mildred shook her head, no. She didn't like to talk while driving over the river. She wasn't afraid of falling. She had no fear of heights. She liked to be alone with the water and the sunlight and remember her Uncle Tommy and her mother and how they used to sing in the car together when they went visiting over in the next county. *Have yourself a merry little Christmas. Make the yuletide gay...*

"Why not?" Dixie pressed.

Mildred didn't answer right away. She took three breaths and let them out before telling her the truth. "Because it's not a riverboat of history. It imitates one. The Harriett II doesn't carry the life and the people and the music or the cargo of original riverboats. Mark Twain wouldn't write about the Harriett II. Oscar Hammerstein would never have written "Old Man River" or any of the other songs from "Showboat" for the Harriett II. What we see there is just a boat on a river trying to recreate a nostalgic part from history. That boat is not the kind that Louis Armstrong rode upon or Mark Twain or W. C. Handy when he was a part of minstrel shows. Riverboats were a vital form of transportation on the rivers and how some traveling performers got around to different places and performed."

"If you were on the Harriet II, you'd be missing Mark Twain and Mr. Handy and who else? What was that other name?"

"Louis Armstrong. He had quite a life. He was locked up for something as a young man, and he learned to play the horn. When he got out of jail, his horn and his music took him all over the world."

Dixie leapfrogged again.

"So why do you like that song? Have yourself a merry little Christmas song?"

Mildred did not tell Dixie the deeper truth when she answered. She did not tell her, 'My mother used to sing that song, and I could feel such a longing in her when she sang that song sitting over in the passenger seat of Uncle Tommy's car while I watched and listened from the back, and no, it is not a hymn, but when Mother sang it that song became a prayer'. Mildred didn't tell Dixie that.

Instead she said, "I saw the same movie you did. I like "Meet Me in St. Louis." Mildred wanted to tell Dixie that the movie was based upon a series of stories by Sally Benson who wrote "Junior Miss" columns and how Sally Benson had also been recruited to co-write the dark Alfred Hitchcock movie "Shadow of a Doubt," but she didn't have the chance. There would be no one else Mildred Budge could ever tell that to and add: "Imagine writing sweet junior miss columns and also dialogue for an Alfred Hitchcock thriller. Imagine being a person who could do both."

"I don't like Judy Garland," Dixie stated flatly, staring out the window.

"Some people don't," Mildred replied as they reached the shore on the other side of the river. "Judy Garland lived a tragic life."

"Everyone does," Dixie said, but there was no self-pity in that proclamation. She wasn't whining either. She was just offering a point of view. "Whether you can see Jesus or not, life is kind of tragic."

"Is it?" Mildred asked, her voice almost a whisper. Nothing about her life felt tragic to her. Every day was rife with meaning, prayer, work, and often joy. For deep inside Mildred Budge a coursing joy ran through her, and if she hadn't been such a well-trained, well-behaved church lady, it would have shown more on her face. But Mildred Budge was very well behaved. So were the other Bereans, and when they joyfully sang Christmas carols, they were all so very well-behaved together. In that very moment, Mildred Budge wondered if the good behaviors of well-trained church ladies were almost tragic. Almost. She would have to pray on it.

"It's been a while since I made this drive," Mildred said, repressing her thoughts about her sister Bereans and the way they sang so softly together—not making enough noise to bother anyone down the hall or cause the preacher concern should he walk by while they were singing and wonder, 'Are the ladies getting too loud?' Avoiding offending the preacher or an elder was a part-time job for Southern church ladies. Mildred wondered if there was ever going to be a retirement from such an occupation.

"There used to be a kind of child's playhouse that looked like a fairy princess castle on the left side of the road." Mildred said, zigging and zagging in the rhythm of Dixie and finding a kind of comfort in the movement. "And that's what's left of it," she said, tipping her head left in the direction of where the princess playhouse had been once upon a time long, long ago.

But no little girl or princess would live in what was there now. What remained was ugly—a dark dome— a hut with scales. It had been discolored by age and pollution. There was no sign at all of a log cabin. The last one must have been sold long ago, and only this distorted version of a fairy tale castle remained.

"It looks more like the kind of place where a troll would live than a princess," Dixie said. "It needs a bleach bath."

Why hadn't they buried the poor thing? If Mildred hadn't seen what it was originally, she wouldn't know what it was now. *Yes, a dark hut for a troll.*

"It does," Mildred said, as they passed a sign on the left where a woman lived who told fortunes. She had been there for years. The fortune teller had regular customers who depended upon her. There was a sign in her front yard inviting people to come inside and find out their futures.

As if reading her mind, Dixie asked, "How do you suppose people like that are still in business? Who goes to fortunetellers anymore?"

Very, very lonely people who will pay someone to hold their hand...

"People who want to know the future," Mildred said. *Very, very lonely people who will pay someone to hold their hand and look at the mythical lifeline of their palm and make them feel significant by seeing something that isn't there. Any lies will do if you are really lonely.*

"People get born, live a while, and then they die," Dixie replied. "That's the future. If they've been good, they go to heaven."

"Not really good," Mildred replied. She couldn't help herself. "They don't become angels either."

"I don't want to discuss *it* today," Dixie said emphatically.

Fountain City was suddenly upon them, or they upon it. Real businesses appeared. Gas stations. Hair styling shops. Tire stores.

"Don't get all Jesus-y on me again," Dixie warned. And then to change the subject, Dixie asked, "Do you know where Main Street is?"

"I used to," Mildred replied truthfully. She wasn't looking for an argument. She also couldn't prove that she knew exactly where Main Street was by declaring the number of turns and blocks it would take to get there. Instead, Mildred drove steadily under the speed limit, past the welcome sign to Fountain City, and continued to feel her way along, a right turn here, another turn, another turn, her left foot repeatedly tapping the brake.

"Do you know where you are going?" Dixie demanded.

"Sort of," Mildred said softly.

"That must be wonderful," Dixie replied enigmatically. "I envy you."

7

WHERE IS MR. FIXIT?

"I see a lot of cars down there on the left," Mildred reported, squinting. Morning light was hard on cataracts. Evening light was gentler but still challenging. Car light at night was the worst. Starbursts of light assaulted your eyes when the headlights of approaching cars hit the windshield. In that moment, Mildred was glad to be able to see cars parked up and down Main Street.

Traveling at the speed that would get her pulled over by a cop who believed she was going too slowly, Mildred searched for a convenient parking spot, although any place she picked would require backing out onto Main Street traffic later when they were ready to leave. Mildred dreaded backing up.

"Is that the pie shop?" Dixie asked, pointing, oblivious to the dangers of parking on Main Street.

The music box shifted in her lap when her hand moved. Dixie caught it quickly, casting a quick glance in Mildred's direction. *Did you see I almost dropped it? Would you hate me if I did?*

"It must be," Mildred said, ignoring Dixie's close call while spying a less congested parking spot five spaces down from the lit-up pie shop. "I'm going to park as close as I can to the pies, and then we'll figure out which side your Mr. Fixit is on."

"He's not my Mr. Fixit," Dixie said, reading the words on the window of a snack bar that wasn't open yet: Soda Fountain Coke Floats $1.

It was dark inside—no lights at all. It was almost eleven o'clock. Retail stores were usually open by 10 am. Small town stores were different, though. Small town stores opened when their owners could get there. Shoppers who were primarily their neighbors and friends knew the routines of the town and made allowances for funerals, school meetings, and other civic matters. The owner could even have kinfolk visiting from out of town, and everyone would know that. Small town neighbors wouldn't expect a dollar Coke float if the owner's kinfolk were in town.

That's where Mildred parked, filing away the idea that the shop with the soda fountain might open before they were finished, and she could treat them to Coke floats. A Coke float for a dollar might make the trip worthwhile. Mildred didn't hold out much hope for any other result with the pies or the music box.

Dixie saw the same sign about the Coke float, and it triggered a memory. "I sat at a soda fountain years ago in New York City and flirted with a stranger. He thought I was French until I answered his 'Bon jour' with 'Howdy.' We laughed and ate a bowl of chili together. It was good chili."

Mildred repressed all of the unpleasant associations she now had with chili, attempting to focus on the important information revealed. Dixie had known a life in New York and been enough of herself—unified in her personhood—to have flirted with a stranger and to remember that flirtation in the present moment as her most dominant self. From a different woman, the confession would have elicited some comment from Mildred that resembled a like revelation: "Me, too. I've flirted in my day. I've had a love of my own." Mildred knew how to murmur small revelations based upon bare facts that had far less importance in reality than they sounded like they did through confession.

Out of the car, Mildred pressed the lock button on the remote. Then, she pressed it again, the horn blasting twice in the morning quiet of Main Street.

Dixie froze in place, waiting to see if Mildred was going to test the door locks a third time. Mildred felt

Dixie's attention and jammed her keys securely deep inside her purse. Twice was enough.

"Do you want me to carry the music box?" Mildred asked, stepping carefully up on the curb. She looked for a parking meter, but there wasn't one.

"Why haven't we come over here before? It's very nice," Dixie said, holding the music box tightly--her answer to the question.

"It is," Mildred replied. "Do you want to go that way?"

"Why do you always ask questions when you are really giving instructions?" Dixie said, turning toward the pie shop.

"I used to be a school teacher. That's how I talked then, and I haven't gotten over myself yet," Mildred answered simply, but she had also learned that technique from Fran who was a great sheep herder with her questions.

"Stop for just a minute," Dixie said. "Or maybe I should have asked, 'Do you want to stop for just a minute?'"

Mildred stopped. She studied Dixie carefully. She wasn't sure what was going to happen. "Are you all right?"

Dixie nodded, her eyes blinking in the sunlight and her fingers gripping the music box so tightly that they were white at the tips, all the blood pressed out of them. "Don't you ever just want to stop for a minute and take in the life around you? I mean, look, this is a very nice street. There are lit-up snowflake decorations hanging on the lamp posts. The air feels good and fresh, and across the street—but why must we hurry? —there's a pie shop with all kinds of possibilities inside. We don't know what they are yet, but we will soon. And," Dixie added with a rueful smile, "You know as well as I do that when we go inside, we are going to face a bunch of pies. We are going to want them all, and choosing just one will be a hard decision to make. But we will have to choose a pie. Don't you get tired of having to pick only one? Haven't you ever wanted to say, 'Bring me some of the best ones, and I'll try them all?' Before we do, before we go inside and face all of that, let's just stop for a minute before life gets harder than this. Complicated, I mean. I love this place. I love Fountain City." Dixie announced.

Turning her face up to the sky, she closed her eyes, and breathed the sharp wintry air. She was quite a sight standing there on the street in her long green shorts, knee-high striped socks that matched her red and white striped shirt. Her Christmas necklace had stopped blinking sometime during the car ride.

Companionably, Mildred Budge closed her large brown eyes too and breathed. The muscles across the tops of her shoulders relaxed. The tension in her right jaw loosened. 'Why am I gritting my teeth?' She wondered. Her purple corduroy pants suit was thick enough to be cozy, and she was concerned again by how underdressed Dixie was for the chill of the day.

"I haven't had a piece of pie in a long time," Dixie confessed suddenly. "You and I have been making fruitcakes. And at home when I want something sweet, I eat cookies. Vanilla wafers."

"Fruitcake," Mildred agreed. This year's experiment in making Christmas fruitcake had been disappointing and expensive. She and Dixie had made little loaves of them the week before with hard, chewy store-bought fruit for the homebound people and then delivered them. Her victims had received the small fruitcakes one and all with resignation and glazed expressions: 'Fruitcake again?'

Mildred knew her fruitcakes were disappointing, but she had not been able to solve the problem of them. They should be good, but they simply weren't.

Mildred was on the verge of giving up her quest to create an edible, delectable fruitcake that tasted the way Christmas was supposed to taste. She had been trying for years. For years she had given up, only to pick up her quest the next year or the year after that. In this way and in so many other traditions and annual quests that Mildred couldn't leave behind, Christmas had become a lot of work.

"So, do you want a piece of pie this early in the day? You've hardly had breakfast," Mildred said.

"Now that is a real question—not instructions masquerading as a question. Most certainly I want pie," Dixie replied emphatically, moving ahead of Mildred toward the crosswalk and the small square sign in the shape of an old-fashioned doily on the front door that read: Welcome Saints and Sinners! Mrs. Bopp's Sublime Pies.

"You have to really know who you are to describe your own pies as sublime," Mildred observed, pausing to see if Dixie wanted to stop and absorb another perfect moment.

She didn't.

Dixie pushed open the door and went right on inside, letting the creaky wooden door slam toward Mildred, who instinctively raised a hand and caught it from hitting her in the face. The weight of the door jammed Mildred's right pinkie finger backwards, and pain surged up through her elbow. Just that quick, genial good will for Dixie turned to irritation.

Mildred stifled a curse word just as Dixie said upon entering, "Hallelujah and praise the Lord! Coffee and pie all over the place!" she said delightedly. "I wonder if it's chicory coffee."

Even though Mildred was standing three feet behind her, Dixie spoke as if she were close beside her. "I had a cup of coffee in New Orleans once that tasted as good as coffee smells, and I have always believed that it must have been the chicory. But who knows? I might have just been in a good mood that day, and there was a man on the street playing a love song on his trumpet that I like—it was 'La Vie En Rose'-- and I was sitting under a big blue umbrella eating warm beignets covered in powdered sugar, and the coffee came in those big white mugs you see in old movies, but you don't see those cups anymore. Maybe they weren't dishwasher or microwave safe and got thrown out when electronics made life so much faster. I miss those big white cups," Dixie said in a great gush of exultation. "Once upon a time you could drink good coffee in a big white cup!"

Mildred wiggled her right pinkie, and it worked. The pain evaporated as suddenly as it had arrived. So did the anger. Mildred smiled with a determined heart. It was worth the trip to see Dixie experience such delight over something as simple as a pie shop.

The coffee did smell good. Mildred moved inside the front door, vaguely aware of something rotating slowly over her head. She was just about to look up and confirm that a slow-moving ceiling fan must be rotating above, when a man she had never met came up behind her, gripped her by both shoulders, turned her gently toward him, and kissed her soundly on both cheeks.

He kissed her like a debonair Frenchman in an old movie.

Like he was glad to see her. Like he was really glad to see her.

Like Mildred Budge had never been kissed in public before.

"Merry Christmas, Sweet Cheeks," he said, his eyes laughing at himself and her and looking past Millie at Dixie to see if she needed to be kissed and her shoulders thumped too.

Dixie's eyes widened in horror, and she stepped back, clutching the mute music box in front of her for protection.

The Kissing Bandit didn't take offense. Instead the man, who was dressed in a navy business suit and sporting a red Christmas necktie with a reindeer on it, raised his right hand to greet the lady who was watching from behind the counter filled with pies. Ignoring the ancient brown spinet piano banked against the right wall, he walked directly to her and asked, "What's good to eat this time of day, Beautiful."

"You tell me," the pie lady said, pointing to an array of small plates with bite size samples of different pies

69

for customers to try. She wore a thick olive-green sweater under a red and green ruffled apron. Stenciled on the front was the message: "Have a sublime day and a piece of pie."

Then as the insurance salesman (that's what he looked like to Mildred Budge) chatted amiably and sampled pie bites with Mrs. Bopp in private, Dixie moved toward the closed piano and Mildred followed her. Mildred was jarred. It had been quite a while since anyone had kissed her, not once but twice, on both cheeks, his warm breath brushing across her surprised parted lips as he greeted her.

Involuntarily, Mildred raised her right hand and pressed the first place on her cheek where he had kissed her and then the place on the other cheek, wondering what had brought on such a rambunctious show of affection for a stranger. *He must have mistaken me for somebody else. Probably a touch of dementia,* Mildred concluded. Increasingly, the explanation of a touch of dementia was the muttered solution for a number of mysteries of life. *Ah, well....*

"You were under a kissing ball. See there," Dixie said. "You were standing right there asking for it is what happened. Do you need to wash your face? I know how you are about germs. You're forever washing your hands."

"I am?" Mildred asked. Did she wash her hands so much that others took notice and thought she had some kind of germ phobia? She looked at both hands. The skin was dry. She did lotion them a couple of times a day and before going to bed. Her legs and arms, too. Mildred had concluded that aging was drying her out. But maybe she was bathing excessively. The thought troubled her.

"I think I'm all right," Mildred said, as she took a step backwards and brushed against the closed piano.

"I'm Edwina Bopp. You girls make yourselves at home," Mrs. Bopp called out. "I'll be with you directly."

And when Mrs. Bopp looked right at Mildred Budge, she suddenly, inexplicably knew the truth. Dixie was right. Mildred did want to wash those two kisses off her face. She was about to look around for the washroom when an older, settled man with a gentle bearing materialized in the doorway on the back-left side of the room. He wasn't dressed for baking or even washing the dishes. The man with a reliable steady gaze was wearing old-fashioned, well-washed, faded blue denim overalls—the kind men used to wear on trains when they were guiding it on its track, one elbow resting on the small open window while behind him carloads of passengers trusted his ability to get them to where they needed to be. Yes, the man who had emerged through the connecting doorway looked like a train conductor.

He smiled at Dixie first. Then, Mildred.

"You two girls looking for me?" Mr. Fixit asked.

8

WE NEEDED A KISSING BALL

B efore they could answer, Mrs. Bopp spoke up. "They're in my pie shop. What makes you think they're not here just for a slice of sublime pie?"

"Because something's broken, my love," he said, with a kindness in his eyes that was so powerful it pulsed from the light in his friendly gaze to Mrs. Bopp, whose face became transcendent with the realized joy that the wiry older man in front of her adored her.

And then that warmth pulsed over to where Mildred and Dixie were standing. Dixie took the first step toward him and then another, forgetting Mildred, moving toward the affectionate gaze of Mr. Fixit as if the light from his eyes had created a tractor beam that held and drew her.

"My music box is broken," she said, a little girl's voice coming from an older woman's frame and body. She grew smaller in her elf costume.

It never ceased to surprise Mildred—that voice, that sound, inside an older woman. "Can you fix it, please?"

"We'll find out soon enough," he said, nodding toward Mrs. Bopp, who gave him a look that meant a hundred things and one unmistakable confession: Love you, honey.

Mr. Fixit pointed to the narrow connecting doorway through which he had entered the pie shop. "I'm Buddy Champion. The light's better in there in my shop," he promised, and with a nod to Mildred he waited for Dixie to go through.

"She'll be all right," the pie lady promised immediately, reading something in Mildred's gaze. Whatever the pie lady thought was not anything Mildred could easily explain. How do you tell perfect strangers that your friend has multiple personalities and might leapfrog and zigzag from subject to subject? Mildred consoled herself with the reminder that Dixie had navigated the world of other people long before Mildred had become her friend.

The light in the pie lady's gaze assured Mildred that whatever was worrying Mildred about Dixie didn't need to concern her now. "We're all friends here. Saints and sinners who like pie," she said. She spoke calmly in measured tones while behind her someone else was rustling pans in the kitchen on the other side of the wall. The pie lady had help in the back. Immediately, Mildred wanted to go back there and meet them. She loved visiting in kitchens.

"Don't stand too close to that front door unless you want to be kissed; but if you do want to be kissed, you can stand there all day long and people will kiss you right and left as they come and go," the pie lady explained with a genial smile, as if standing around waiting to be kissed was a perfectly normal and socially acceptable choice to make. Her hands moved automatically to the back where her apron was tied, and she tested the knot.

Mildred didn't know what to do. Their reason for coming had gone with Dixie and the broken music box into Mr. Fixit's adjoining shop next door. Dixie said she wanted pie, and her friend Mildred couldn't eat pie without her. So, Mildred was left standing by a silent piano wishing she could wash two kisses off her face, and what was a closed-up piano doing in a pie shop anyway?

The pie lady was arranging pies behind her counter. Mildred spied steam from pies right out of the oven. They smelled very good, and Mildred was hungrier than she had been when she and Dixie had started out on their pilgrimage with the broken music box.

"Once these pies cool, I've got to get them boxed. The lads are coming for them," Edwina said more to herself than to Mildred.

The old man called out from his shop, "Do you need me, Edwina?"

The pie shop lady turned, her hands at rest among the pies. "Not yet, Buddy."

"You feeding the power line crew again today?" he asked, loitering in the connecting doorway.

Mildred would soon learn that Buddy's pace was to come and go, come and go through the connecting door from his shop into hers and back again. It wasn't restlessness. It was something else.

The pie lady nodded. "They wanted the shepherd's pie again, so that's what I made."

His lively gaze grew interested.

"I know you like it. There's a shepherd's pie reserved for you in the back for whenever you want it," she promised.

Mildred Budge had heard of shepherd's pie but never eaten one. She knew enough to imagine that the top was going to be creamed potatoes, most likely brushed with melted butter, and baked over a savory meat mixture. She could almost tell what the spices were from sniffing the air. Simmered beef seasoned with garlic powder, onion, and something else.

The pie lady read Mildred's mind. "What do you think it is?"

"Onion. Garlic powder. Dale's steak sauce?"

"No. Worcester, but just a few drops. Everything you said and some Kosher salt and Mediterranean black pepper. You really can't make shepherd's pie wrong. I use only ground sirloin. If you know how to make beef stew and creamed potatoes, you can make a shepherd's pie. I do like to play with the spices and other flavorings though, and I only make it for cold months. It isn't a summertime pie."

In that moment Mildred wanted a shepherd's pie more than she wanted the music box fixed. More than she wanted to be alone. More than she wanted that reindeer ornament of Prancer that she had stupidly made herself walk past, living with the ridiculous resolve that you don't have to own all the pretty Christmas ornaments that you like. Sometimes--yes! -- sometimes you could have a reindeer ornament of your own and a shepherd's pie. Mildred tried not to think about the Elvis ornament, but it had been awfully cute, too.

The pie lady understood and shook her head. "The lads placed their order yesterday because they said they needed it to look forward to, and I've been looking forward to thinking about them eating my pies. I made just enough for them. But I've got a chicken pot pie for the general p...." Mrs. Bopp stopped short of saying *public*, shaking her head as she substituted the words, "My neighbors. And there's a lady over at the assisted living home six blocks thataway who has a sitter. Deborah comes over pretty often and gets two lunchtime individual pies from me for them. One of these days I want to go over there for a good visit. I can't leave here easily is the problem. I need to hire more help. You're not looking for a job, are you?"

It flashed through Mildred's mind that she could have all the pie she wanted if she worked in the pie shop. Only she'd have to give up her morning meditation time to drive over the river, because it was late morning and the counter was already full of pies. You didn't make that many pies by not getting to work at the crack of dawn. Mildred was up at the crack of dawn most every day, but she was reading her Bible and praying and staring out the window, wondering what was going on in the universe. Still, for a flash of a second, Mildred Budge was tempted to take the job on the spot. Oh, the intoxicating sensation of being desired for any reason. To be asked! To be wanted! Why that was wonderful! Even better than getting kissed twice while standing under the kissing ball in the doorway.

Mildred drew closer to the pie counter and Mrs. Bopp. "No, I'm not looking for a job, but if I were, I could work here," she said truthfully.

"You and I would get along. I can see that as plain as day. I'm Edwina Bopp. I used to make miracle fudge, but now I make sublime pies. This is my shop. And that fellow who has gone in the other room is my friend. My very best friend. Is the girl with the music box your friend or your sister?"

Mildred nodded *yes* to both questions, and said, "I am Mildred Budge." She stopped, for through her life she had introduced herself a variety of ways. I am Mildred Budge, a writer of devotionals. I am Mildred Budge, a fifth grade school teacher now retired. I am Mildred Budge, the friend of Fran Applewhite, and she and I manage two booths over at the local antique store, though it's not really about antiques.

That morning, Mildred Budge said her name, and leaning forward, her cheeks still burning from the kisses, said, "And I have always had a love affair with small town bakery shops. I see many pies," Mildred affirmed, ignoring the other lady's easy references to miracles and the sublime.

Southern women didn't use the words *miracle* or *sublime* very easily. Mildred stole quick glances at Mrs. Bopp to see if she was holding back a laugh or any kind of idea in her eyes that would explain the phrases *miracle fudge* and *sublime pies.*

The other woman's gaze was open and welcoming, sweetly familiar.   Mrs. Bopp wore the friendly trustworthy gaze of a church lady, the kind of older woman who attends Sunday school and church regularly; and when they are all together, Sunday school ladies unapologetically call each other girl.

"If you have a sweet tooth you can try what I like to think of as my breakfast pies—custards, sweet potato—and then later in the day, and I don't do it very often, I might make a chocolate fudge pie or two for people who come by for afternoon coffee.

"But I have to be oh-so-very careful about that because when people hear the words *chocolate fudge*, they automatically believe I have adapted my miracle fudge recipe into a pie, but I have not," Mrs. Bopp stated flatly. "You can make a fudge pie that is simply sublime rather than life-changing. Miracles happen so fast, and there are times when we need to move more slowly. That's what I think. We all need to be still from time to time, and the right pie can help you sit quietly in sublime repose and muse about the small things of life, which so often go unconsidered. I can still make my miracle fudge whenever the occasion calls for it; but when I do, I call it miracle fudge. I don't pretend it's something else."

"Like a sublime pie?" Mildred asked, going suddenly still as she understood immediately what the other woman meant. Sublime silence. Sublime attention. Sublime focus on what was right in front of you. And what was in front of you was worthy of sublime gratitude.

"Right you are," Mrs. Bopp agreed, reaching over the counter to pat Mildred Budge's hand that had come to rest on the edge of the top shelf of the display counter.

Mildred almost apologized--almost said, 'I'm sorry. I wasn't thinking. I wasn't going to touch your pies with my unwashed hand. I've taken to resting where I stand with my hand touching a surface. It helps me keep my balance. I don't know how or when I got to where I thought I wasn't steady on my feet. I've always been steady until I began to do that--reaching out to touch something solid to keep myself in place in time and space.'

But Mildred didn't say those words. They weren't necessary. Mrs. Bopp was only patting Mildred Budge's dry hand. Being sweetly welcoming. *Hello there. Welcome.* It wasn't a kiss on the cheek twice. It was a pat on the hand, twice. *Pat-pat.*

Standing in the doorway, Buddy listened. He spoke up like a commentator at a ball game explaining the action on the field. Mildred was surprised he was there again—had thought Edwina's Buddy had gone back into his small room where Dixie was waiting with her little girl voice and her broken music box, and right then, Mildred's own hope ignited. She so hoped Mr. Fixit could make the music play and help the angels fly.

His standing there at loose attention between his shop and the bakery meant something else this time.

It seemed like he simply wanted to welcome Mildred in his shy way of coming and going—to prove he hadn't run off with her friend but was glad she was there too. Men made a different kind of small talk than women did. Men loitered differently. They waited differently.

"Folks come by and pick up a pie on their way to work or to share at the office for lunch. A lot of people come get them to take to sick folks. It's got everything you need to stay alive right there in one pie," he promised, his body turning toward the light of his work room and Dixie and the music box.

Mrs. Bopp nodded for him to go on. Maybe that's what he was waiting for—a nod from the pie lady. He smiled, turned, retreating into his man cave, his footsteps a gentle falling, soft and kind in their farewell. Mildred saw that everything about Mr. Fixit was kind and gentle and that his farewells were never rejection, just a temporary absence that wouldn't last for long.

"That nut pie is left over from yesterday. They're half price. I don't know why I didn't sell out yesterday. That doesn't happen very often. God's way of keeping me humble. Thank you, Jesus. Or I just overbaked. I hate to have left-overs."

"Dollar a slice," the man called over his shoulder, selling his lady friend's pies. "Can't beat that."

"Hot chicken pot pies for lunch today," she said, repeating herself. "And people around here eat lunch around 11, and they'll be along shortly to pick one up to take home. I've got to go check the ovens," she said with a start and looked over at the old man who had come back just that fast.

Dixie was with him now. He motioned for her to sit on the small bistro chair across from him just inside the pie shop. The table was beside a blue quilt hanging on the wall with a shining Christmas Star stitched into it.

Buddy situated himself in the opposite chair now holding a huge lock attached to its hinges that had a screwdriver stuck in the keyhole.

Edwina Bopp explained. "Buddy will help your friend in a minute. Harry Reid is having a barn door emergency. That's the lock off his barn door. It got jammed with that screwdriver, and now my sweetheart is supposed to get that loose. He'll figure it out, or he won't."

"Did he put up that kissing ball?" Dixie asked.

"Yes. It's funny you should ask that. Sweetie Pie thought of that kissing ball. He hates it when I call him Sweetie Pie. He prefers Buddy." She feasted her eyes on him for a few seconds and then continued with her explanation. "There was a lot of kissing happening on Main Street. People fall in love in Fountain City all the time. You could trip over a bride and groom out on that street any day of the year. I mean, really. Love is in the air as abundant as the underground springs that break through all over this county."

"Underground fountains?" Mildred asked. "That's right. I've heard about the springs. That's why everyone calls you Fountain City."

"It's a prettier name than the one we've got. But names don't matter."

"The kissing ball?"

"We put it there to control how much kissing is done in here—not to encourage more. People were staying put, not going to work, not living their lives. They were just sitting in here smelling the pies cook and telling Buddy their problems. In between that they were kissing and whispering sweet nothings to one another. It got to where my six small tables were full all the time. We weren't meant to be that kind of establishment: eating pie and canoodling. No one wanted to leave.

"There was even some talk once upon a time about calling in a preacher to conduct a group wedding and simply use my shop for the reception because, well, the refreshments are already made if you like pie and coffee or ice tea.

"I thought about tearing out the door and expanding into Buddy's shop, cause it's not like he's not here all the time, and we could use the floor space for some more tables. That's when he told me to hold my horses and found me that kissing ball to hang in the doorway.

"He was inspired by a kissing ball hanging in a doorway at Sue Luckey's house last Christmas. No one was using it, and when he said something like that, sweet Sue kissed my old darling right in front of her husband Ron. Then she climbed up on a chair, took that kissing ball loose from where it was hanging, and gave it right to him. Sue Luckey is very generous and flexible. She is an Episcopalian, and Episcopalians are known for being able to climb up and down whenever they need to do that. They are more flexible than, well, other people. I love that about Episcopalians. Sweet Sue only used the kissing ball at Christmas, but we keep it up year-round. Anybody needs to be kissed while they're waiting on a piece of pie just lingers there for a while.

"So, now the kissing happens coming and going under that kissing ball. And it's good for lonely people. It's especially good for girls and boys who never get kissed."

As if Mrs. Bopp hadn't explained anything at all, Dixie said, "I'd like one of your recipes for miracle fudge. Buddy—he said I could call him Buddy-- was telling me about your miracle fudge. Said miracles happen when people eat it. So, I'd like the recipe, although to be perfectly honest and above board with you, I've never had much confidence in recipes or Bible verses to make miracles."

Mrs. Bopp's brow furrowed at the coupling. "The key to experiencing a miracle is being willing to change, often, very fast. I changed. I used to be unable to give away a recipe for my fudge because I always thought I could make it better. I had to get over that, I'll tell you. I learned my lesson. I put out a lot of fudge and pie recipes over there underneath those two slightly rusty cast iron skillets no one seems to want. And when I make a different version of a pie, I throw out the old recipes and put out the new ones and go on with my life. Somebody came in here once and asked me for a recipe from three pies ago, and I didn't even answer them. I told them if they were going to come in here with questions about old recipes to go over there and stand under the kissing ball until they couldn't think about it anymore. Kissing's good for that, too. They had the fool kissed out of them.

"The kissing ball has worked pretty well. The current recipes are over there on the table. Sometimes, the fellow who owns the newspaper comes by and picks up a random recipe and prints it in the newspaper and calls it news. He asked me for a photograph of my pie one time—one time! —and I told him, 'Go stand under the kissing ball until you forget what you just said—until you are over wanting a snapshot of a pie that has long ago been eaten by somebody else and is now only a sweet memory of theirs, not yours. Let it be a memory. Don't long for the past that is gone and wasn't yours to begin with, for goodness' sake. Live your own life.'

"He never asked again, but the truth is, as soon as I was ready to share recipes, nobody wanted them as much anymore. It's only when you don't want to share something that people think they have to have it. I think that's one of the basic problems people have with the gospel. It's free, and people who are used to paying for something or being told they can't have it simply don't value what is free and readily available."

"Do we want a chicken pot pie for lunch?" Dixie asked, changing the subject. "Buddy said that his lady was making chicken pot pies for lunch. He said she uses celery and mushrooms."

Mildred didn't want a chicken pot pie. She wanted the shepherd's pie cooked with ground sirloin and Worcester sauce. There were no more shepherd pies, except the one reserved for Buddy. That reserved pie is the one Mildred wanted badly.

"You know the answer to that simple question," Dixie stated. "Why don't you just say so?"

9

YOU DON'T HAVE TO EAT
PIE TO GET ALONG WITH US

"You don't have to eat a pie just to get your music box fixed," Mrs. Bopp said. "Sweetie Pie over there will help you after he gets that bolt unstuck. Poor Harry Reid is having a barn door emergency this morning. I said that already, didn't I?" Mrs. Bopp shrugged, undisturbed to be heard repeating herself.

"His barn door is wide open, and he can't lock it back up until Buddy gets that lock unlocked. Harry took off the lock and brought it in because Sweetie Pie wouldn't drive out there that far. He can't bear to be away from me." Mrs. Bopp stared at the slightly rotating kissing ball, lost her focus for a moment, and in the losing of her focus, smiled.

Mildred turned to assess Mr. Fixit sitting at the table by himself wrestling awkwardly with the screwdriver. Sweetie Pie's glasses were sitting on top of his head, and his slight weight did nothing to testify to the goodness or the sublime-ness of the pies on the counter or the others in the oven in the back. He was a lean wiry man who liked to work with his hands, and he was in love with a plump woman who liked to cook.

Mrs. Bopp settled three small pies in a double-thick brown paper bag with a piece of carboard in the bottom to support the weight and folded the top carefully. "Your pies will be all right to get home if you just hold them steady," she promised, passing the bag over to the man who said he was taking home lunch to the wife and her sister Lucille, who had come for a visit and now, bless her heart, she wouldn't go home.

"I've got it," the man replied stoutly, taking possession of the large bag with his three sublime pies. He turned toward Buddy, who was concentrating now. Dixie was waiting. Mrs. Bopp was watching. Harry Reid needed his lock fixed.

"I came this way looking for the fix-it fellow. Got sidetracked by the smell of these pies. Why isn't Mr. Fixit over at his shop where he belongs? I knocked on his front door first before coming over here, but nobody answered it. I wanted to ask him something."

There was a tedious whine to Mister Man's voice; he wanted more than the steaming pies that Mrs. Bopp had packaged neatly for him.

Mildred had heard that mewling whine in a lot of people's voices from time to time. She heard it right then and vowed privately to God that she would never use a whine to get what she needed or wanted from someone else. She wouldn't even whine to God. That last idea came to her out of the blue, and it startled her. Mildred was warm enough in her purple corduroy pantsuit, but a shiver went through her when she realized that she had whined to God in the past. Immediately, she could name a dozen occasions in the recent past when she had done exactly that. The church lady shook her head to clear away the jolt of that surprise.

Mrs. Bopp was non-plussed. Whining customers, like happy ones, were regulars, and she smiled genially. "People know where Buddy is if they need him. You can go over there and ask him what you want to know. He can hear while he works with his hands."

The offer softened the nervous man who shifted the shopping bag with his pies, placing one of his hands under the sack while the other gripped the folded top.

"If you're sure I won't be bothering him."

"Buddy doesn't mind people talking to him while he fixes other things. That girl with the music box is ahead of you though."

That girl was Dixie, and she was shivering. Every time the front door opened, a blast of cold air came inside. Whatever her theory about weight loss, Dixie the elf was now regretting she hadn't dressed more warmly.

The man walked over to Buddy and waited for the old man to look up at him. Buddy's gaze stayed on his hands and the screwdriver and the lock.

"If keeping your shop door locked is a way to get your lady friend some pie-selling business, it worked like a charm. I've done bought three of the little pies." Mister Man's voice was too loud for the room.

Mrs. Bopp's face grew sad when her customer said those very words where everyone could hear them. Mildred fought rising, going over, and taking the man and his sack of pies by the elbow and escorting him to the door. The atmosphere of the pie shop had been perfectly pleasant before he came inside and would be again after he left.

"What's worrying you?" Buddy asked neutrally, priestlike. He didn't wait for the answer, however. Laying down the lock, Buddy stood, exited quickly, rummaged around in his shop on the other side of the wall, and returned holding a man's tan insulated jacket. The lining was a cheerful red and blue plaid flannel design that Mildred's Uncle Tommy used to wear. People who had known and loved Tommy bought him neckties with that plaid.

Mr. Fixit draped the over-sized jacket around Dixie's shoulders and leaned down and whispered something in her ear.

Dixie's gripped the front sides of the jacket close together tightly across her chest, looking up gratefully. The expression in Dixie's eyes was one that Mildred had never seen before.

Mister Man sat down in a small nearby bistro chair, situating his sack of pies on the table top across from Mr. Fixit at work and took a deep breath.

"Go ahead," Buddy invited. "What's on your mind? I can hear you while I work."

"It's about my vacuum cleaner," he said, and his voice had grown less angry having watched the exchange between Mr. Fixit and Dixie.

Buddy nodded that he had heard. "The vacuum cleaner is one of the great inventions of the 20th century, but I'm not so sure about the 21st. I think there are people loose in the world inventing all kinds of sweeping up machines. I heard tell of one of those robot vacuums coming on in the night and scaring the lady who lived there. Thinking the sound of the robot vacuum cleaning was a burglar, she locked herself in the bathroom and called the police. They broke down her front door and found the poor lady cowering in her bathroom, hiding from a vacuum cleaner. I don't know anything about those robot vacuum cleaners."

"I don't have all day..." the man said, interrupting Buddy. And then realizing that he was sounding irritable in a room where everyone else was at ease, he stopped himself, and said, apologetically, "I don't have one of them."

Buddy recognized the struggle for help and how asking for it cost some people more than others. "Do you have the machine out in the car?"

The man didn't want to say yes or no to that question. Mister Man didn't want to commit to paying for help until he knew what he could expect. Instead, he explained, "There's a burnt place in the cord. The vacuum sucks up good enough, but I'm wondering if the house is going to catch on fire."

"Not if you don't use it," Buddy said, finally looking up. His eyes were smiling. Just smiling.

Mildred saw the smile in Mr. Fixit's eyes and made her second prayer to God in the same five minutes: 'Always make my eyes smile at people who have meanness in them. It will help them.'

"I thought about putting some electrical tape across the place where the wires are exposed," the man said, and his voice was growing too loud again for the room.

"Did the cord get really hot when you did that?" Buddy asked. His smiling eyes grew concerned. Cautious.

94

"I said I was thinking about it."

Buddy grinned, and the smile was enough to prompt a confession.

"Okay. Yes. I wrapped a little piece of black electrical tape around the scorched part. But it feels hotter than it should. Too hot."

"Do you want me to take a look at it now?" Buddy asked, standing up, ready to interrupt his work to help this man.

"I need to go drop these Morning Glory pies back at the house before I go back to work," the man said, picking up his sack with pies.

"Morning Glory pies?" Buddy asked, giving Edwina such a look.

"That's what she called 'em," he said. "I tasted a sample. Tasted pretty good. Kind of like a chicken pot pie."

"Sometimes she calls them that, too," Buddy said, leading the way to the front door. "I'll walk you out and look at your machine in the car. No charge for a curbside consult," he promised.

Turning as he left, Buddy motioned to Dixie, asking, "Will you look after that lock for me?"

Dixie sat up taller and scooted her chair closer to the lock.

The customer was pleased with Buddy's extra effort. He began to speak, passing under the kissing ball without an upward glance. No one tried to intercept him—give him a farewell kiss or a good luck kiss or even a I'm-glad-you're-leaving kiss. "Because it's kind of not a very good vacuum cleaner to begin with, and I don't want to spend too much money getting it repaired. It might be smarter to buy a new one,"

"But you'd rather not spend that kind of money this close to Christmas because your wife wouldn't think that a new vacuum cleaner is a very good present."

"Ain't it the truth!"

The pie shop became soothingly quiet while Buddy was outside looking in the trunk of the car at the problematic vacuum cleaner. The man placed his sack of pies inside on the front passenger seat. Then Mildred saw Buddy easily lift out the vacuum cleaner and massage the cord up and down with his fingers.

The two men talked, both nodding, their bodies slightly turned away from one another.

Buddy came back in holding the vacuum cleaner just high enough to keep from rolling it on the street. But once he was inside, Buddy lowered it and rolled it on the floor next to the small table where the lock was sitting frozen and still useless under Dixie's protective gaze. "Honeybun, I told our new friend Charlie that he can pick up his vacuum cleaner on the way home from work this evening, and you were going to throw in a free full-sized dinner pie for his supper. It just needs a new cord."

"Then it's going to be your shepherd's pie because my other pies are spoken for, and just because I had leftovers yesterday doesn't mean I'm going to have pies go begging today. And furthermore..."

"There's always a furthermore," Buddy said with a wink at Mildred. His eyes lit up while the pie lady explained the checks and balances of fixing things and sublime pies.

"You think I'm going to mind you calling me Honeybun, but I don't care Sweetie Pie. You just call me anything you want, but you need to help these two girls with their music box when that lock is unstuck. They have been waiting patiently."

"She's done," he said, pointing toward the repaired lock. "Harry can come for it anytime. Just had to wiggle that screwdriver out and tighten up that thingamajig inside."

Dixie asked, "Is it my turn now, Mr. Buddy? Can you fix my music box?"

"If it can be fixed, I can fix it," Buddy replied sunnily, before peering into Dixie's eyes, where what he saw arrested him.

For a moment, Mildred stopped too, while the motions of pie selling and serving customers continued. The phone rang and Mrs. Bopp answered it, her voice sounding different.

Mr. Fixit confronted the music box while asking Dixie, "Now, tell me the whole story. Where did you find such a magnificent treasure?"

10

WE FOUND THE MUSIC BOX
AT A DEATH SALE

"We found the music box at a death sale. It was in a box marked children's toys. We just bought it for fun."

Mildred stared in wonder at Dixie. Dixie had not been with her. The label had read "Mystery Box" not children's toys. Dixie had seen those very words 'mystery box' when she cut open the tape. The event had been an estate sale, not a death sale, though, Mildred considered the idea, *death sale* was sort of true. That phrase was the only accurate part of Dixie's report.

Did Dixie know she was confabulating?

"This isn't a children's toy," Mr. Fixit said respectfully, rotating the music box slowly around to see all five sides. "This is a work of art. That's what this is. You got yourselves a gen-u-ine work of art."

Dixie placed her left elbow on the table and leaned forward, cupping her face in her left palm, considering the man in front of her. Her teeth still wanted to chatter in spite of the warm jacket she was now wearing zipped closed over her elf costume. "What else do you see?" she asked intently.

It was a real question, not the kind of questions that Mildred Budge and so many people in daily conversation asked as a form of small talk, filler, and stalling. Self-protection. Deflection. From time to time--not always-- Mildred's questions were a kind of picket fence built around herself. Dixie's question was real: *What else do you see?*

"Edwina, do you have some fresh coffee back there?" Buddy called out before answering.

"You don't want to drink coffee. It'll make your hands shake," Mrs. Bopp replied. "Your hands need to be steady. You want a mug of warm apple cider with a cinnamon stick or a glass of decaffeinated ice tea."

"Don't you tell me what I want. If I say I want coffee, I want coffee," he said.

'This is what love sounds like,' Mildred thought. 'This is how love can sound.'

"Do you want coffee?" he asked Dixie, sharing a conspiratorial glance with the self-proclaimed owner of the music box, excluding Mildred altogether. "It'll warm you up. Don't drink the cider. It's too sweet and will ruin your appetite for any kind of pie."

Dixie shook her head, clasping her hands in her lap. In spite of how hungry she was when she left Montgomery, she was not hungry now.

"I have not introduced myself properly. I'm Buddy Champion, and that lady over there is Edwina Bopp, a fudge-making genius who has decided to test herself against the mountain called making sublime pies. If it's not one thing it's another," Buddy said, shaking his head gently, smiling, smiling.

"Just between us...." He began.

"You and everyone else in the room who can hear you," Edwina called out playfully.

Buddy grinned. "Like I was saying, just between us and anyone else who can hear me, I say I can fix anything until I can't fix it. Then if I can't fix it, I just say I was wrong." He laughed. "You have to believe in yourself in order to try. Then if you fail, you just have to accept reality. But for a little while when I say I can fix something, why, even at my age, I'm Superman." His eyes were laughing and so were Edwina's. Dixie's eyes began to sparkle.

The pie lady shook her head mournfully as she placed a cup of steaming coffee with just a hint of chicory on the table beside her near-sighted sweetheart who was telling the story of his life inside small talk. She thought he was a walking miracle of a man, greater than any comic book version of a

Superman. He was real, and he was kind. "Talk on, Buddy of my Heart."

"She never gets tired of thinking up names for me. One of these days she's going to invent a pie, and name it after me."

"If there's sweet potato in it, you won't eat it," Edwina predicted as she placed a steaming cup in front of Dixie. "Just a little warm chicken broth from stewing chickens. Usually, I freeze broth for cooking later, but you need a little hot broth in you right now, dear." She waited for Dixie to taste the savory broth, nodding encouragement while casting glances at the frequently opening front door. There was nothing she could do about the breeze coming inside.

Beside Edwina, Buddy settled down, as if near a warm fire.

Mildred Budge could feel the warmth between them—not desire, not passion only. This was something else. What was between Mr. Fixit and the pie lady filled the room.

Buddy studied Mrs. Bopp as if he were just seeing her for the first time. She wasn't glamorous. She was a little plump, a little soft, a little dated. Her hairstyle was a version from the beauty shop that required curlers, hairspray, and a rinse of some kind that made her salt and pepper hair slightly lavender in the light. Her green sweater under the apron was bought for warmth instead of fashion. The apron with her motto on it had been made by her own hands, the message embroidered carefully: "Have a sublime day and a piece of pie." Her morning's application of Revlon Soft Silver Rose lipstick had worn off, but there was a bright shining light in her brown eyes that made Buddy smile.

Mildred read the expression on Buddy's face, and when she did, she thought, *'Oh my, he loves her so. It is a holy love. And this is a holy moment.'*

And in the seeing—in that holy moment— Mildred Budge was changed. Not just a little bit. Mildred Budge was changed deep down in ways that had never been touched by the light of pure love before. And suddenly, just like they used to do in the movies, Mildred Budge, who had been a girl once upon a time in love with life, wanted to sing in response to what she saw and because seeing a holy love can make you want to rejoice out loud with music.

"I can't be fixed," Dixie announced suddenly. "A lot of people have tried. Nobody can fix me." Her statement was a dare. *Can you fix anything*?

"What's wrong with you?" Buddy asked in the same level tone of voice. Priestlike. Patient. Trustworthy.

Dixie's voice changed right then. A different Dixie arrived. Direct. Unapologetic. Truthful. "Too many people live inside of me. Sometimes, I think I'm a slum landlord with a bunch of sinners who are crashing at my pad."

"I used to live there. It's no fun, is it?"

The question touched her. Nothing Mildred Budge had ever said to Dixie about the brokenness she lived with ever touched her the way Mr. Fixit's question did. *It's no fun, is it*?

Dixie nodded solemnly. "Can you fix it?"

"You?" he asked, his gaze friendly, his hands still holding the silent music box.

"Me," she said. "And it," she added, but she was holding the cup of broth close in front of her trembling mouth and wouldn't meet his eyes.

"I'm going to have to take the music box apart. Do you trust me? It could break worse," he explained, ignoring her other question.

Dixie had expected nothing more. She was used to people deflecting, redirecting, brushing off the biggest questions of hers and anyone's life: *Can you fix it? Me?*

No one could fix her, and the people who claimed to know Jesus the Fixer often held back on affirming the promises made to lost people and wandering sheep.

Dixie looked at Mildred who had also been handed a cup of coffee. No one was in a hurry for her to place an order. "Coffee is on the house. All the refills you want." That's what Mrs. Bopp said. *Coffee is on the house.* A jar was positioned over in the corner on a table not far from the kissing ball, and there were words on the jar: Faith Promise.

A small sign situated on a small picture frame explained its presence: "Throw some money in if you're feeling happy or if you are weighed down by too much money. You can get rid of a lot of your troubles by throwing them away, and money is one of them."

Mildred mouthed the words to Dixie, "Say yes. Let him fix it." And under her breath, the church lady prayed, "Jesus, Jesus, help him fix it. Help him, Jesus."

"Would you mind telling me what you think of this?" Mrs. Bopp asked, placing a small ramekin in front of the praying Mildred Budge. Mildred was surprised to be addressed. She had gone into a kind of silent humming: invisible church lady who prays unceasingly. And then another church lady saw her anyway. But that was true of church ladies. Wherever church ladies were, they always recognized each other.

Mrs. Bopp placed a small teaspoon near the ramekin. "It's just a little recipe I'm working on. It would be a mercy from Jesus if you would taste and tell me what you think about my newest concoction.

Your sister will eat when she's ready. That old man eats all day long. Table scraps mostly. Whatever I put in front of him. Why don't you just sit there and relax a little bit? Nobody's in charge of the world here except Jesus."

'How did she know?' Mildred wondered. She didn't want to be in charge of anything. Nothing at all. *Have yourself a merry little Christmas, and don't make me be in charge.*

"What is this?" Mildred asked, looking at the small white ramekin.

"You tell me," the pie lady dared her.

And then a man came in who said he was with the power line crew.

"I'm here to pick up our shepherd pies," he declared stomping across the floor toward the counter. His boots left a trail of sand and a couple of pebbles that had been trapped in the cleats. Mrs. Bopp pretended not to see, and she willed Mildred Budge, the other church lady present, not to react. *Floors get dirty. Don't worry about it.*

The cooling pies were no longer on the countertop. Mildred had not seen them removed. *When had that happened?* She didn't miss much, but she had missed that.

The pie lady leaned over and picked up a sturdy carrying box with a handle similar to the one Mildred had bought that morning at the estate sale. "Here you go, love. I put in some napkins, spoons, and a batch of my chocolate walnut fudge made just for all of you so that you won't fall off any of the utility poles. Everybody needs to eat a piece," she advised.

"Yes, ma'am," he replied seriously. "We'll all eat a piece of your fudge before climbing any pole. But is the shepherd's pie like last time? That's all any of us wants to know. Is it the same pie?"

Mrs. Bopp's innocent face dawned with a smile of confession and good will. "I never know how to answer that question," she replied sincerely. "But my pies will feed the hungry for a spell. That's not all I hope for, but it is the inspiration of every recipe I serve."

The line man laughed robustly, and in the small room nearby Mildred could hear Buddy talking, and his talking sounded like a lullaby, yes, a lullaby, and she felt—yes, Mildred Budge felt, Dixie is finally listening. Today, she can hear the story of Christmas.

11

WHY IS THERE A PIANO IN HERE?

"Why is there a piano in here?" Mildred asked suddenly after the lineman with the dirty boots left with his box of shepherd pies.

The sound of her own voice erupting like that surprised Mildred. She was usually better at filtering herself.

"It was abandoned by some unfeeling person who probably does the same thing to kittens and puppies!" Mrs. Bopp explained. "As soon as I saw that big old music box sitting out there on the sidewalk—on the sidewalk in broad daylight subject to bad and good weather! -- I rescued that poor thing from the street. That's what happened. Some do-gooder—you could call him that if you want to because people have ideas like that and people like that call themselves idea people-- had this half-baked notion cause it wasn't a thought-out plan to leave a piano out on the sidewalk right next to the street for people passing by to play as they walked down Main Street.

"Any way you look at it, the idea is loco. Plain loco. I couldn't bear the thought of a piano getting rained on. You know and I know, it's going to be rained on sooner or later. When the drops start to fall there won't be anyone nearby with a large enough umbrella or a plastic cover like some people put on their cars to drape over it.

"So, I got my Sweetie Pie over there to help me push that piano in here. And there it sits. I'm not hiding anything. I'm not trying to steal someone else's piano. The man who owns the newspaper and who ran a story on the piano when it first showed up on the street has seen the piano sitting right there. Tom stood right there under that kissing ball and saw this piano—I keep it dusted!-- and when he looked at me, Tom didn't even ask any questions because anyone who knows me knows I'm not going to let an abandoned piano sit unrescued outside my business any more than I would let an abandoned kitty or puppy be left on my doorstep without bringing it in and feeding it.

"Well, like I said, I keep it dusted," she added, almost as an afterthought, but the phrase caused her to look over at the small room where Mr. Fixit and Dixie were concentrating on the broken music box.

"He'll either fix your music box, or he won't. And just between us, if he can't fix it for that girl who has her heart set on it, my sweetheart will grieve. And he'll think about it. And he'll wonder what else he could have done, just like some doctor who meets a patient close to death and can't save him or her from a fatal disease. My old darling feels like that about the things he can't fix. He'll try, and if he fails, he'll grieve. And that's one of the things I admire most about him. He doesn't have to be Superman for me. When he grieves over not being able to help someone, why, he's my hero."

Mildred listened. She was good at listening. And so often people told her stories like the one the pie lady was sharing while outside on Main Street people were going back and forth, and sometimes they stopped to peer in as if they could see from the other side of the glass what Mrs. Bopp had made for the special that day.

Just then a passing shopper waved at Mrs. Bopp, and she automatically waved back, then continued her story, "I thought someone would come for the piano, but no one has. Now it just sits there. It grieves me—grieves me, I'll tell you-- to have an unplayed instrument sitting there. I don't know how to play, and no one who comes in here ever sits down and makes it welcome. Not even a kid, and usually kids will get into mischief with a piano, but not a single child has tried to play that piano. I'm mystified."

"It hurts me to see a silent piano, too," Mildred confessed, lifting the spoon which until that moment had been unused right where the pie lady had placed it.

Mildred was hungry enough to eat anything. But she was also a Southern woman who didn't rush—not on the interstate, not at the dinner table, not even to a silent piano that was calling to her in its silent though demanding way. And now there was this other reason: the woman who made pies felt about the silent piano the way that Dixie felt about the broken music box.

'It's a broken world,' Mildred thought, spooning a delicate bite of the small portion of pie in front of her.

"Take your time now. No rush," Mrs. Bopp advised.

'Music to my ears,' Mildred thought.

She savored the first polite spoonful and retreated inward. One small polite sublime taste, and the church lady was deep inside herself, resting with the Lord in a way that is prescribed in the Bible.

In time out, Mildred directed the small teaspoon again, piercing more deeply the light golden crust again. A rich brown broth contained small bite size pieces of tender beef. She closed her eyes. *Which spices? Which red wine?* She spooned a third get-acquainted taste, closing her eyes to concentrate. When Mildred opened them, she said approvingly, "You have made boeuf bourguignonne in a pie."

"I thought it was a good idea!" the pie lady exclaimed. "But you never know until you try."

"Oh, it's a good idea all right. A very good idea," Mildred said with enthusiasm, and then still resting but in a different tempo, she applied herself to more of the exquisite portion.

Mrs. Bopp's phone rang with a call-in order, and she turned to answer it. "Busy time of day," she explained. But there was no one else in the small pie shop to hear her.

Mildred understood. Sometimes she announced her own actions in her home to no one who was listening, except Jesus. He heard everything. Of that, Mildred Budge was certain.

Mildred was alone with a sublime concoction of saucy beef and red wine that took her to the coast of France. One taste and she was sitting on a beach wearing a billowy cotton dress in a deep blue with white polka dots, barelegged, her feet pulled up as the water rolled in and out just enough to bathe her toes, getting closer, the breeze constant, the horizon stretching out her sensibilities, her awareness, until her experience of physical space had expanded far beyond what you learn is the reality discerned by only the five senses and teach to fifth graders. With the experience of a bustling French village behind her and the call of the horizon in her sightline that had arrived in a small white ramekin and a spoonful of sauce, Mildred couldn't add to her Christmas list or do the work on it. Couldn't bring out the decorations. Couldn't set up the tree. Couldn't try to find her red bird Christmas sweater that she wore on Christmas Eve to the candlelight service, postponing the other question she asked routinely: "Is it time for me to retire my red bird sweater? Is it out of fashion? Am I?"

*****

For three Christmases in a row, Mildred Budge had also been wondering if at least on Christmas Eve whether she should dare to wear at home the dainty mink-trimmed pink satin bedroom slippers that a former student who now owned a string of ladies' boutiques had sent her out of the blue with a card that read, "For walking pretty with Jesus. Merry Christmas, Mildred Budge." It would be such a gamble; she might get them dirty.

Mildred Budge had never in her life envisioned that she would own anything so dainty, so impractical. Mink-trimmed pink satin bedroom slippers were an extraordinary possession. Later, she saw a television show starring that woman who gave away her favorite things as a form of celebrating happy discoveries, and that television lady gave people mink-trimmed slippers like the ones Mildred had received. Those slippers had to cost over a hundred dollars a pair. Sometimes Mildred looked at the expensive slippers during the holidays in the same way she brought out the brass and crystal music box that played 'O Holy Night" to hold and behold ritualistically on Christmas Eve, but she had never worn the satin slippers— couldn't bear to risk getting them dirty.

"I know," Mrs. Bopp said, although Mildred had not asked a question. "I know," she repeated. "It's hard to accept sublime anything. It's a test right there, and you don't have to pass the test. You don't even have to take the test. But if you can sit there and just eat that dish of pie, that's Christmastime really. Just accept the goodness of peace on earth and good will to men and women who have sense enough to say *yes* to the invitation to rest in Jesus. Rest from self. Rest from fear. Rest from sin. Just sit there, and if it's not enough, go stand under the kissing ball. I do from time to time. When I do my Buddy hurries over and kisses me fast, and then he pulls me away. He won't let me stand under the kissing ball without him."

While Mrs. Bopp was talking about love and Mildred was resting intermittently on a beach in France, Dixie and Mr. Fixit had returned to the small bistro table just outside his door and just inside the pie shop. They were together, focused on the music box. He moved between two worlds.

Though he was focused on the task at hand, Buddy was whispering to Dixie and smiling. When he looked up and around, his attention held Dixie close while his hands kept moving, small, gentle movements that created great waves of air that rippled through the room and created small eddies of exultation. Stacks of white napkins ruffled on table tops. The tassels on the thin beige window curtains fluttered. And the kissing ball hanging over the front door rotated on the golden string to which it was attached.

From where she sat so close to the silent piano Mildred could feel the strings inside the closed piano behind her start shimmying, a sweet vibration that she could feel in her back and which traveled up her spine to the base of her neck. In the humming Mildred felt the freshening breeze of the French coastal waters— a foreign land rife with potential adventures! -- and she could smell bread baking, hard crusty baguettes and light, buttery croissants. Everyone around her in their various occupations worked together for the common good and for the glory of Love.

1 2

WHAT IS A FAITH PROMISE?

"What is a Faith Promise jar?" Mildred asked suddenly, without thinking. She had not planned to ask the question. The second question also popped out, like a sneeze that catches you off-guard. The sound of her own voice erupting out of her like that surprised Mildred Budge. One second you're on a beach in France and the next breath you take you are inside a pie shop in Fountain City.

It didn't surprise Edwina Bopp.

"Is it a tip jar?" Mildred asked, rising. She walked over to a broom situated in the corner between the back kitchen and the front room. "I can't stand it any longer," Mildred admitted, taking the broom. No one paid any attention except Edwina, who nodded: "I had almost reached that point too. I almost couldn't stand it any longer. But if you do it, it's one thing. If I do the sweeping, it's another."

A Southern woman never cleans up after a guest while the visitor or another guest can see her work.

That visitor or guest might draw the conclusion that he had made a mess and wasn't welcome. Or feel judged. Or feel like an inconvenience. No. You never clean up a mess where the guest can see you.

"Of course," Mildred murmured. Taking the broom and making small respectful motions, she gathered the trail of sand and pebbles left by the line crew foreman and pushed them out the door. And then because she was Mildred Budge, she went out on the sidewalk and swept the front path clear, shifting the dirt to the curb and then into the gutter.

Two minutes later, she returned, placing the broom where it stayed between jobs. The conversation with Edwina picked up where they had left off.

"The contributions to the Faith Promise jar are old-fashioned, sentimental, and for old time's sake. They go for missions and such. We do that here. It's a lot of fun. People don't say that too much, and they should. Loving other folks can be fun. Giving doesn't cost anybody who does it in the name of Jesus anything. You can't out give God. My preacher says that all the time, and I believe he's right."

Mrs. Bopp heard a beeper sound from the back of her kitchen on the other side. But she didn't rush to it like a first responder to the sound of fire or flood. She stood still, and when she did the daylight outside changed and poured through the two front windows, blanketing them all in a warm basking glow. A lazy grin spread across Mrs. Bopp's face. "Don't you just love Christmastime?" she asked, not exactly to Mildred— to the world, really. To herself. To Buddy, who wouldn't hear the question until later after the sun had set.

Then, after the passing of time and moonlight had replaced the sunlight, the question would reach this man who was her sweetheart, and Edwina's Buddy would reach across the supper table and cover her hand with his and say, "Oh, yes. Oh, yes. I just love Christmastime. Now. Here with you."

And Edwina would know all that he meant by that faith promise. It was a lullaby, a prayer for tomorrow, an echo of the hallelujah chorus, a wedding vow in the making. She would know everything he meant and much of what Christmastime could be, and everyone around them would know too—or at least enjoy a small piece of sublime pie.

Before Buddy ever said it, Mildred heard the question and his reply that had not been said out loud yet. In that way she experienced Christmastime with them in that rare event of time travel called eternity, which people didn't mention much. "Oh, yes. Oh, yes," Mildred said. She heard her own voice, but the words were startling, coming out of her like that, and then she smiled and thought, 'I shall wear my pink satin slippers with mink trim this very Christmas Eve and watch something with Bing Crosby in it and sing every song Bing sings right along with him. Yes, oh, yes.'

Mildred Budge didn't know it yet, but the new Christmas song that would be distinctly hers was inside her now. That Christmas song "Oh, yes. Oh, yes," would hum inside of her for days to come and long past the burdensome change from one year to the next when the event of midnight was supposed to feel magnified and different: auspicious, and which never had been and never was like the moment she was having in the pie shop while the pie lady in charge was in the back opening the oven door and checking to see if her crusts were brown enough and Mr. Fixit was close enough to talk to about your problems and who would try to help you if he could.

And then wonder filled Mildred's voice. Pure wonder, and Mildred whispered to the lady who couldn't hear her and she didn't want her to—not really, 'You're alive. You're alive. He's alive. Right now, Dixie is alive, and she can hear that man speaking while he works on the music box, and I'm in the middle of all this bustling creativity and sharing and resting and loving each other in the name of Jesus. And Dixie has the help she needs. I only needed to bring her.

You did the rest. You did the rest. And you're doing the rest in me because you don't stop until you have finished what you started.

'Outside on Main Street, people I didn't know were alive are alive, and I love them. They are going to important destinations bearing sublime pies to commemorate life itself with precious friends, wives, visiting sisters-in law, and fellow workers who need them.' Mildred's prayer trailed off and would pick up again when the Spirit moved her.

Buddy's movements snagged Mildred's attention. Reality was like that. The motion of human life often called you back from prayer to a present moment to see what was happening.

Mr. Fixit fished a pocketknife out of his pocket and was fiddling with the assortment of miniature blades inside. He chose one and went into a zone of concentration that was like the conductor of a symphony instead of a train. Mr. Fixit was hearing only his music—his thoughts about the music box-- and everyone else was outside his concentration. Except Dixie. She could hear Buddy's music, and he could hear hers. For the first time in her life Dixie was abiding next to someone who knew who she was better than anyone else had ever known who she was, and Mildred was relieved because she had not failed. Good works were appointed for you to do before you were ever born, and in that moment, Buddy was talking with Dixie about coming home. Mildred heard those words plain as day, and Dixie could hear him too. It was Christmastime, and it was the right time to remember that Mildred Budge wasn't in charge of the world or of fixing Dixie.

But something was going on.

Something good.

And it wasn't just pies baking all day long.

13

HARK! YOU JUST NEED TO PAY ATTENTION

The front door opened and closed again every few minutes. There were a few people talking around Mildred Budge, but the drama in the pie shop was focused on Mr. Fixit and the music box and the child who looked like a woman who was sitting beside him watching intently, listening raptly. Dixie was warm now from the jacket wrapped around her and the steaming chicken broth the pie lady had given her.

There was more silence than conversation, and the silence was punctuated by deep sighs of contentment from people coming and going or taking a time out to sit by a small round table and eat a piece of pie until suddenly, and without any expectation that it was about to happen, the music box made a noise. One wouldn't call it music exactly. But there were three notes at least.

Mildred instinctively sang the three notes to herself quickly, in the same way as when a rare snow comes you go outside and try to catch the first snowflakes in your open mouth. The three notes didn't lead to the name of the song. Even so, Mildred searched inside her memory for the song itself. "Doe, me, so," she sang inside herself, storing the gaps between the musical intervals. Those three notes did not bring forth a song—not even a distant memory of some elusive melody. She was intrigued. For Mildred Budge was privy to one of the biggest secrets that routinely happened out loud in her church.

The pianist often began the call-to-worship prelude with a few notes from secular songs and then transitioned into the hymn of the moment. But Mildred Budge was sure she had heard the opening strains of "St. Louis Blues," "Rhapsody in Blue," and other songs from the American songbook that the pianist included like a call to pay attention before she played the call to worship. Mildred recognized those songs, and she kept the pianist's smiling secret because no one else seemed to notice.

But in that moment with the music box being resurrected and its song called forth to testify that once upon a time a composer's work had been kept safe there, she could not name that tune. Rather than be frustrated, Mildred Budge smiled. She was delighted to hear a new song.

Dixie pivoted quickly and stared at Mildred, who nodded that she had heard the hopeful notes. The slender wooden Christmas tree in the center of the music box had been lifted off and was balanced on the tips of its limbs positioned carefully on the tabletop. Mildred was afraid to look at the five naked angels. She hoped they hadn't been nicked or scarred, bless their hearts.

Dixie made the *okay* sign and nodded her head vigorously up and down. She mouthed the words, "I told you he could fix anything."

But Mrs. Bopp's Sweetie Pie hadn't fixed anything yet.

"Here's part of the problem," Buddy said, reaching into the box with his gnarled work worn forefinger and thumb to extract a significant sliver of wood.

"It's a big splinter," Dixie called out.

Mr. Fixit held the thin piece of wood up to the light as Mrs. Bopp came over to see what he had found.

"It broke off from something in there and got lodged inside the mechanism. This little plank stopped the music."

"Will it play now?" Dixie asked. She was sitting tall in her chair, both feet on the floor, her hands clasped in her lap.

"Only one way to find out. Do you want to do the honors?" he asked, turning the box with the brass key in its side toward Dixie. "Go on. It won't bite," Buddy urged. "But don't turn the key too hard."

Dixie held his gaze. "I break things. I always have. I'm famous for breaking things," she whispered, looking around to see if anyone else could hear.

Because I am so broken myself.

She didn't say the words, but Mildred felt the words the same way she felt the vibrating piano strings in the closed piano.

Mildred heard the confession. *'Did she? Did Dixie break things worse than other people broke things? Or did she feel a kind of nameless guilt about breaking things because she was so broken herself?'*

"Just be gentle with it and yourself," Buddy coaxed. "Just take the key between your two fingers and turn it just so. Just so," he repeated for emphasis. "Gently. Gently."

"Maybe she needs to eat a little something more first," Mrs. Bopp called out, protectively. The other church lady could sense the tension. She didn't want some kind of emotional emergency to happen in her little shop. For any grown woman who went out in public wearing an elf costume that wasn't warm enough in the winter was a frail creature, and others who cared to look could see it. Mrs. Bopp could see.

She turned and traded knowing glances with Mildred Budge, who nodded that she shared the other woman's concern.

Dixie was unaware of Mrs. Bopp's concern or of Mildred's relinquishment of responsibility of her to Mr. Fixit. The only voice Dixie heard was Buddy's.

Trusting him, Dixie reached out and grasped the small music box key gently between her thumb and forefinger.

"Hang on just a minute," Buddy said suddenly.

"Let me put the tree back in its place first. Maybe the tree needs to be situated on top. Sometimes the weight of something else settles the innards down. Sometimes that's true."

Dixie pulled her hand back. Buddy nestled the wooden tree back onto the golden turntable of the music box. "I'll wait until later to put the screws back in and tighten it. That ought to be enough. Let's see if it will do something now."

"Now?" Dixie held Buddy's gaze attentively, expectantly.

Around the room others who had been paying attention to their pies stopped to witness what might happen next.

Dixie reached out and with careful, slow motions grasped the brass key on the side of the box again.

This time she turned it, her eyes closing in a squint as she concentrated.

"It's okay," Buddy said. "It's been a while since those little gears moved. It might take a little effort." Speaking under his breath, he said, "Where's my oil can?"

Mildred instantly remembered an oil can of her youth and how she had routinely oiled the chain on her bicycle. *"Oil makes the world go around,"* her father used to tell her. *"Or at least the wheels on your bike."*

When she no longer rode a bike, he would tell her, *"Love makes the world go around."*

It had been a long time since Mildred Budge thought any maxim or cliché could sum up the human experience in such a way that it would make you want to turn a key on a music box to hear what it might play. But in that moment, Mildred agreed with Mr. Fixit that he needed his oil can. Because while Mildred wasn't as curious or as hopeful about the music box being repaired and the music it might play, Dixie was and Mildred Budge wanted Dixie to have what she wanted. Surely you could have some of what you wanted during Christmastime.

A solution to a problem.

Some music instead of silence.

The experience of an old man whose reputation for fixing things was true.

Order to be established.

Jesus. Jesus. Jesus, Mildred Budge prayed. *You came to fix what Adam broke. Fix this. Fix her. Fix me. Fix this broken world.* It was Mildred Budge's Christmas prayer that she prayed all year long. And today she was seeing Buddy be the hands and feet of Jesus. Edwina, too.

"Try again," Buddy said. "This time, be a little firmer."

"Now?" Dixie asked. And her hand moved. One more gentle twist. One more twist and Dixie stopped, pulling her hand back and positioning it in her lap.

Nothing happened at first. A breath was taken. Just one breath. Everyone took one breath. And then the music began. Slowly. The same three notes they had heard before repeated, but more tinkling notes followed. Slowly.

A waltz?

A carol?

A hymn?

A strange and lilting piece of music moved through the room like a breeze rustling the top limbs of evergreens. Mildred Budge was immediately transported to treetops. Yes, the song was an evergreen hymn of praise.

The music was short-lived. Stopping. Then starting again.

This time the eight bars of this foreign song were familiar. Just barely. But Mildred sighed as the notes fulfilled their measures, and from those notes, she could predict what the next measures would sound like. For a whole song was often stored as clues in the introduction, moving from that sweet beginning to a kind of romantic middle that arcs back to the ending that brought resolution. Sweet satisfaction. Oh, my. Oh, my. Mildred Budge smiled a new smile. It was not any version of any church lady smile she had ever worn before. It was a brand-new creation of a smile, and like the song from the music box that was now inside of her, the smile was hers forever. The idea made Mildred's eyes sparkle and her toes curl. They tingled with a desire to stand up and move.

Dixie leaned forward and turned the key again.

14

A REMEMBERED REST

FOR CHRISTMAS

The music started again, and while it played, customers continued to come and go, scanning pies, sampling pies, choosing pies, leaving or choosing to stay after stopping to kiss one another beneath the kissing ball. Mildred sat against the wall near the piano, her small beef pie finished. While she was inside the rest of Jesus, another ramekin with a different sample was placed nearby. "Taste this, and tell me what you think. You're a fine taster. I can see that plain as day."

Mildred looked questioningly at Edwina Bopp.

"It's my idea of butterscotch pudding—filling-- with a different kind of crust. Just butterscotch. Just pudding. I know it's sort of early in the day for such shenanigans, but it's not so sugary as you might suppose from the name, and I think—I could be wrong—but I think it might be good. Not sublime yet.

Not by a long shot. But good. I hope so anyway. You tell me."

"Warm pudding sounds just right," Mildred replied, taking up her spoon again to taste and see.

"It's a shame we don't have the whole song," Edwina Bopp said to someone. Not Dixie. Not Buddy. Not Mildred. *Was she talking to a customer or herself*?

That's when Mildred found the gingersnap cookie crust at the bottom of the warm butterscotch pudding. Oh, sweet Christmas. Sweet Christmastime.

Mildred tasted while Buddy worked, taking very small bites and eating slowly, the new song simmering inside of her. She kept her eyes closed and savored the sublime warm butterscotch made with cream and brown sugar and something else. She didn't know what the something else was, and she didn't want to ask.

Mr. Fixit took out the small jeweler screwdriver about the size of the one Mildred used to carry in her purse to tighten the screws in her eye glasses before she lost it. He tightened the fasteners that secured the tree in the middle. His hands tested the gold lacquered star cresting the top. Then his hands moved to each fat angel, to each instrument. Like a mechanic checking under the hood of a car, Buddy's fingertips ran underneath the lip of the gold turntable upon which the scene rested, testing for something, touching everything.

"Is it fixed?" Dixie asked. "Is it really fixed?"

"You tell me," he said, sitting back. He picked up his cup and took a sip. "Coffee's cold," he announced.

Edwina shook her head and came to the table. "Your coffee wasn't cold when I brought it to you."

He looked up at her and smiled. "Don't make me kiss you right here in front of everybody."

"You are spoiled rotten," she said crossing the room to pick up his cup. He took her hand in his as it reached for the cup and brought it to his lips.

"I am," he agreed. "But as long as you are the one doing the spoiling...."

"You're going to have to eat something in a minute. You haven't eaten anything all day. I've got a shepherd's pie for you back there."

"I want one of those red wine and beef pies you gave your new friend over there," he said, pointing toward Mildred. "She liked it."

"You liked the shepherd's pie the last time," she reminded him.

"That was the last time. Aren't you the one who is always telling me not to be tied to yesterday's pie? I want today's pie. The one that girl over there ate. She liked it. I could see sublimeness all over her face."

"I've never had shepherd's pie. What is it?" Dixie asked, settling back in her chair. She was still looking at the music box. It had gone silent. She wanted to say something, but she wasn't ready to do that yet. She was making small talk about a pie instead.

"Depends upon who is making a shepherd's pie," Edwina said, looking at her kindly. "You need to eat a little something. I can see that. I'm going to bring you..." she promised Dixie, but she didn't finish the thought. Edwina couldn't finish the sentence.

Turning to Mildred, she asked, "Do you need something while I'm in the back looking for what that other girl needs?"

"I'm just sitting here between heaven and earth," Mildred replied sunnily. "It's Christmastime."

Mrs. Bopp stopped in her tracks and grinned as if what Mildred had said was the most interesting reply she had ever heard. And then, though Dixie and Buddy were waiting, Mrs. Bopp went right over to Mildred and took the chair across from her. "I'll be with y'all in a minute. I'm going to take a little time out. A little Christmastime with this lady right here."

And with that, Edwina Bopp joined Mildred Budge at her table and sat with her legs stretched out in front of her as if she had all the time in the world. "What would you be doing if you weren't sitting here?" the pie lady asked.

"Working on my to-do list."

Edwina smiled. "I've been working on my to-do list all morning. You have inspired me, sitting there like you are. I like your present to-do list better than mine. I'll get you some more coffee in a minute."

"I'm not used to people waiting on me. I can get more coffee myself," Mildred explained. But she was in no hurry—no hurry at all.

"Coffee pot is behind the counter," Edwina said, pointing, and in the pointing, the pie lady relinquished one kind of hospitality for another: *Make yourself at home, why don't you?*

Mildred stood and took her cup with her to the back of the counter where the coffee pot was sitting on its compact brown stand.

Edwina sipped her coffee. Mildred joined her. They sat in musing silence together, like old, old friends.

Buddy had taken Dixie and the music box back through the small arched doorway to his shop again. He had that vacuum cleaner he needed to fix. Mildred had lost track of how much time they had spent in the shop. *Had Harry Reid picked up his barn door lock?* If he had, Mildred had missed that. She felt like Harry was an old friend now, and she had never met him, but she wanted to—wanted to wish him from the bottom of her heart: "Merry Christmas, Harry Reid."

"What are you going to do with that music box?" Mrs. Bopp asked.

"I haven't thought that far ahead. I bought it blind at an estate sale. My friend Fran and I manage a couple of booths over at the Emporium in Montgomery. It's a place where vendors recycle used goods, and sometimes we call those used goods antiques. But that is often a stretch of the imagination. That music box is different. It is truly vintage. I think that music box may be more expensive to buy if we charge what it's worth than people who shop our booths will want to pay. And we leave our merchandise there unguarded, and it's the kind of item that could be picked up and walked off with. I don't know."

"Don't you just love those words 'I don't know'? I try to say them as often as I truthfully can. What a mercy from Jesus to be able to say those words. How freeing! But, of course, if you embrace that idea you have to speak up when you do know something is true. Jesus."

"Jesus," Mildred repeated. "He is real, and the Bible tells the truth about him."

"Ain't it the truth," Mrs. Bopp confirmed. "Who's the lady with you? I called her your sister, but she's not really your sister," Mrs. Bopp said, leaning forward. Her left hand reached behind her and rubbed the small of her back. "I wear my tension right there," she said, stretching. "Even when you have the peace of God, you can still have tension in your back."

"Ain't it the truth," Mildred replied companionably. She carried her tension in the base of her neck on the left side from where she tilted her head to see through her bi-focals. She was always trying to find the optimum angle to see better. *Maybe when the cataracts were removed it would be easier to find her focus. April would be a quieter time than Christmas to be inconvenienced by that procedure. Yes, April would be a better time.*

"She's not sure who she is. Her name is Dixie. She has identity issues."

"Don't we all?" Mrs. Bopp said. "I used to make miracle fudge until one day I couldn't make it anymore. I just lost my will to do it. And right up to that point I made my miracle fudge with great zeal— loved making the fudge for Christmas around here. And then one day I didn't want to make it anymore. Felt unfaithful to the town. Kind of unfaithful to myself. It's awfully hard to change when other people don't want you to stop being who they think you are. Or who you've always been."

"Or who you've always been to them," Mildred added solemnly. "It is hard to stop being who everyone thinks we should be all the time," Mildred said. "Sometimes you have to help people forget."

"Ain't it the truth," the pie lady agreed as Dixie reappeared without Buddy.

15

THE MORE THE MERRIER

Dixie emerged from Mr. Fixit's shop and crossed over to the small table across from the piano where stacks of printed recipes were placed free for the taking. Two cast iron skillets functioned as paperweights on top. Dixie randomly collected some miracle fudge and sublime pie recipes without stopping to read the ingredients or how long it would take to prepare any of the dishes.

"Your friend needs to eat," Mrs. Bopp said. "But I don't know what she needs. I usually know," she said with a wistful smile. "But today, for her, I do not know." She smiled at the confession.

Rising, the shopkeeper returned to the other side of the counter while Dixie perused the free recipes.

Mildred called out to Dixie. "You about ready to eat something?"

As if she hadn't understood the question, Dixie said, "He had to take off the Christmas tree again. He said there's something else wrong. The angels should circle the tree when the music plays, but they don't move. I could tell that I was getting in his way, so I came back out here."

Mildred watched as Dixie made a slow rotation around the room, and as she stopped here and there to admire the picture of a red bird on the wall, a blue quilt with the Christmas Star in the center hanging next to it, and the hand-carved nativity scene in the storefront window, Mildred saw them through her friend's eyes. There's a red bird painting. There's a baby-size quilt with the Christmas Star. There's the nativity scene in the window that has no lights at all. No artificial snow. No reindeer. It was an unspectacular tableau.

Eventually, Dixie made her way back to Mildred, placing the collection of recipes on the table between them. She hadn't read them. She had picked them up randomly because she was restless and bored. Dixie didn't cook.

"You ate something," Dixie said. "I'm hungry, but I don't feel like eating. I thought I would want to eat a whole pie, but I don't. I've lost my appetite. I got those recipes for you. There are two dirty skillets on top of them. I was surprised to see rusty skillets here."

"Those two skillets are looking for a good home, but so far no one wants to take on the task of cleaning them," Edwina called out from where she was wrapping up another Morning Glory pie for a man who was trying to hide inside his hat and coat. Just a little bit of his face was showing.

"These recipes have got other people's names on them. Guin. Sue. Lori. Jennie. Twinkle. Twinkle?" Dixie repeated, ignoring Edwina's comments about the frying pans.

"Twinkle. I'm sure she did at one point. Someone called her that, and the name stuck." The statement reverberated inside of Mildred and reached the pie lady, who nodded knowingly.

"I'm surprised you serve other people's recipes for pies," Dixie remarked. "I thought this was your pie shop."

Mrs. Bopp's face changed then. It turned into light, and the colors of her being were radiant with a golden aura that Mildred thought was how marketers used to advertise face powder, but they had stopped. She didn't have to look any closer to know that Mrs. Bopp didn't wear face powder. Edwina Bopp wore light.

"When I first opened up this place, I thought I would be serving my own creations. I truly did. And I still invent pies right along. But then I began to hear my customers talk and some of them—not all—were reminded of an old recipe someone else used to make, and they missed that someone. They wanted to share that pie again as a kind of living memorial that said, 'A part of my heart is with you in heaven, and I remember you now and eat a little pie with you from time to time.' That's what I heard, and so I began to tell them, 'Bring me that recipe for holy remembering, and I'll make it. That's Julie Ann's sweet potato pie with a streusel topping that I'm baking today. She said it's her mother's recipe. You need the streusel because the filling is so light; you need a bit of a crunch. Fortunately, I have access to some mighty fine pecans. There are a lot of people out there creating beautiful experiences for others, and no place to share what they have invented, want to make, and don't want to keep to themselves. I help friends express that part of themselves."

"So, this pie shop is yours, but you're serving other people's pie recipes," Dixie concluded. Her voice was tinged with a kind of watchful skepticism as if she were reconsidering the pie shop's integrity, its place in society, and whether she wanted to eat a pie named after someone else or not.

"The more the merrier," Mrs. Bopp replied easily.

"The more the merrier," Dixie repeated, with a start of quizzical wonder: *could that be true? The more the merrier*? and then she turned to Mildred, who was listening for the music box under Mr. Fixit's guardian care in the other room. She heard another note. Then another note. The music played again, but now the elusive melody was happening in the background of life in the pie shop. Just that quickly the music box's song had receded and become the soundtrack for the people in the pie shop who were having a kind of Christmastime together.

"What's he doing?" Mildred asked quietly. "I thought he fixed it."

"He said there was something else he needed to check. And then he mentioned glue."

Protecting Mr. Fixit's need for space and time, Mrs. Bopp kept talking. "The men who whisper their pie recipes to me that they don't want others to know were from them are all labeled Honey's Pie, in case you're curious."

"What happens when someone brings you a recipe for a pie that's not very good?"

"In their early stages—their youth-- pies are like children," Mrs. Bopp explained patiently. "They just need to grow up some. I help a pie grow up when it's necessary because I don't serve bad pie," Mrs. Bopp replied readily. "But sometimes people bring a pie for me to taste to prove how good it is, and it's not so very tasty. Out of respect for their deep feelings, I experiment and try to figure out a way to make it better. Sometimes, it's just more or less sugar. More or less butter. Chocolate covers a multitude of trespasses. And then I serve it with love in my heart."

"What has been your biggest challenge?" Mildred asked. She had a number of pie failures in her repertoire: any filling that required a double boiler was a problem for her and more than once she had scorched caramel and milk.

"Rhubarb," the pie lady answered easily. "Although blueberries have their own texture challenges. I like rhubarb and strawberry together, but rhubarb alone and mistreated can get a little stringy."

"I've been working on a fruitcake recipe for years. It's never been very good." It was Mildred's third spontaneous utterance that day. She hadn't talked so much in such an unguarded way in years.

Mrs. Bopp eyed Mildred thoughtfully. "I know a dozen recipes for fruitcake. Maybe more. And none of them is sublime."

16

A CHRISTMAS STOCKING
FRUITCAKE SOUNDS GOOD

"I believe that the real problem with American fruitcakes lies with those indigestible gelled concoctions of hard-to-chew fruit bits some cooks believe they need to buy to stir into what could have been a perfectly acceptable cake batter. That cheap store-bought stuff kills a fruitcake every time and maybe some people. I know for a fact that once upon a time some local morticians used to give fruitcakes to large families who had regularly sought their services through the years," Edwina recounted.

"No!"

"Yes," Edwina said, nodding solemnly. "Death and fruitcake often feel like they go together."

"They shouldn't. Fruitcake should be as festive as Christmas," Mildred argued weakly.

"We should think on it. Maybe even pray," Edwina suggested.

As if she hadn't heard the last sentence, Mildred confessed softly, "I've been using that gummy fruit they sell everywhere in my fruitcakes."

The pie lady looked away out of respect for Mildred's feelings.

"I see it everywhere. Everywhere. And I was duped. I believed because it was everywhere that those colorful tacky globs of gluey congealed color belonged in fruitcake," Mildred said.

"You're not the first, and you won't be the last," the pie lady predicted. "But now that you know what the bigger problem is, you can solve it. There are better versions of candied fruit, but the kind sold on most grocery store shelves is an example of fruit rind abuse."

Dixie and Mildred sat up straighter.

"I'm not kidding. Candying fruit is an art that requires patience. When done wrong, candied fruit can explode in the process, and even as it is drying out, it must be rehydrated from time to time with syrup, and you simply must use a good syrup. There are better candied fruits available that are made from higher quality fruit and saturated in richer syrups. You just have to know where to find them."

"And who makes the good kind?" Mildred asked intently. She was deeply intrigued, for years of failing to produce a good fruitcake did not mean that she was

146

defeated. It just meant she was patient and persevering, both traits considered a fruit of the Spirit.

In that moment the two ladies who had just met became dedicated to solving one of the great mysteries of the holidays: how to make a delectable, digestible Christmas-y fruitcake.

"Let's say we have solved the problem of finding an edible and perhaps delicious candied fruit. What are you thinking about the batter?" Mildred asked.

"We want a substantial batter that can hold our real fruit in a real fruitcake. A part of me wants to consider a couple of tablespoons of cornmeal."

"I know that Southern woman part of you, and I recognize the appeal of cornmeal. But would it blend?" Before the other woman could nod yes or no, Mildred added, "And let's not bake it in a cast iron skillet either. There's a real trend to try and bake everything in a cast iron skillet, and I do love a cast iron skillet, but I don't want my fruitcake to have..."

"Too crispy a crust." Edwina nodded succinctly. They were in perfect accord. "Those two skillets over there on top of the recipes do not mean that I intend to bake a pie in them. They are there because I do not want to clean them. Whoever wants to clean them can have them. In the meantime, they are holding down the recipes. I put them there so people could lust after them."

"I lusted after them," Dixie confessed readily.

"They are yours if you want them," the pie lady promised before returning to the discussion of a potential fruitcake recipe. Mildred was listening and nodding, thinking her own thoughts about the batter and where in Montgomery she could find a better candied fruit. Perhaps she could candy her own fruit. The idea appealed to her. The Boy Scouts sold fruit by the case this time of year as a fund-raising project for their troops, and she could get her hands on some good oranges and grapefruits.

"We can let the cornmeal go and the cast iron skillet, but down the road, some year, some Christmas, it might be fun to make a fruitcake fritter."

Mildred's eyes widened, and not just because she loved the word fritter. A fritter for Christmas sounded very appealing. "I very much like the idea of a fruitcake fritter topped with brandied cherries and set on fire," Mildred admitted readily.

Edwina's eyes sparkled. She nodded, tugging on her left ear as if that were a private signal and promise between them. "In the meantime, what do you think about sugar?" Edwina asked.

"Dark brown sugar," Mildred said without hesitation. "And maybe—just maybe-- and I'll be the first to confess I don't know why the following words

148

are going to come out of my mouth but here they come."

"Speak to me," Edwina urged, leaning forward.

Dixie rose and went over to the two cast iron skillets. She picked one up in each hand and returned to the table. "These are mine," she stated flatly.

"A tablespoon of molasses," Mildred suggested.

"A little bit of molasses goes a long way…." Edwina reminded her, nodding to Dixie that she had heard her. *Of course. Take the skillets. You're doing me a favor.*

"I'm going to put these in the car," Dixie explained. "I need the car keys."

"But the way molasses tastes is worth the gamble…." Mildred replied, nodding to Dixie and passing her the keys. "Come back," she said automatically.

"I know a cookie that finds its whole identity from molasses, and that taste is part of what we want for a sublime fruitcake," the pie lady said with authority.

"Any cane syrups?" Mildred asked. "A friend of mine's husband is a big believer in cane syrup. He thinks it has health benefits the way some people believe apple cider vinegar is a cure-all. He also fancies a certain brand of mayonnaise."

"It is a rare man who understands there are differences between cane syrups and mayonnaise, and who knows what the benefits are even if that is only a shared taste for the same mayonnaise inside a long and happy marriage. That girl is a lucky woman— the woman married to a respecter of cane syrup and mayonnaise."

"His name is Jonathan," Mildred said, though where that memory and how she was able to think of his name all of a sudden like that puzzled her. She had gotten to a stage where she could not always readily remember the names of her friends and her friends' husbands.

"We could consider a tablespoon of cane syrup but only if we decide against that tablespoon of molasses," Edwina replied as she pulled out a small stenographer pad from under the counter and began to write down the named ingredients. "Depending upon how much molasses you use, any addition of dark syrup would be redundant and weigh down the batter. Yes, it would weigh down our cake batter.

"The ideal fruitcake should evoke a Charles Dickens' Victorian England Christmas with hand-knitted red stockings hung from large mantles over brick fireplaces, and in the other room are excited children unable to sleep because they want to find their filled stockings and are thrilled to find juicy navel oranges and cinnamon candies and..." Mrs. Bopp began to see the story of an ideal fruitcake, and

Mildred listened, aware that the woman was beginning to create a fruitcake that would one day be sublime. It might take Edwina years to perfect it, but Mildred had confidence that Edwina Bopp, who had begun her professional life as a chemistry teacher and was now experimenting with ingredients for sublime pies, would persevere. The next evolution in her creative nature appeared to be making a sublime fruitcake, and its creation was important.

The recognition of significant creations is what church ladies share in so many ways that to name them all would take the length of one Christmas to another.

"And this fruitcake would cause people to remember that the event of it—part of its holy origins is that it testifies to the glories of abundance on earth given by the Father of Lights. Every good gift comes down from the Father of Lights. With this fruitcake we would taste and see that a part of the lit-up glory of Christmas is being surprised one more time by the goodness of everything. Everything," Mrs. Bopp said with satisfaction. "There's a verse about that in the Old Testament in that book in the Bible that is so hard to spell."

"Deuteronomy," Mildred interjected. There were many hard words to spell in the Bible.

Mrs. Bopp flinched. "Yes. That's the one. Who can spell it?"

Church ladies never one up one another, so Mildred Budge, who could spell Deuteronomy, simply smiled and nodded that she understood the struggle. It is so hard to maintain a reputation for being an excellent Christian if you can't reliably spell or even remember some of the names of the books in the Bible.

"But the verse I'm thinking about has something to do with experiencing cursing or blessing, and the key to blessing is to be grateful for everything. Be grateful for the abundance of it all. That's the taste of a blessed fruitcake. It should prompt gratitude for the abundance of everything."

"You want a lot from a piece of fruit cake," Mildred said with a grin she usually restrained and released mostly in polite versions of various smiles. Mildred Budge had a smile of encouragement. A smile of recognition. A rueful smile of forgiveness of trespasses because man is made of dust after all. A smile of tender hope. Smiling politely is one kind of church lady response. Grinning is another. Mildred grinned unabashedly with mischief in her eyes, and if an artist who had painted the faces of the angels on the music box could have seen the glint in that church lady's eyes, he (or she) would try to capture it and put that

sparkle and that unabashed grin on get-well-soon
greeting cards for sick people to see when they first
took them out of the envelopes. That sparkle and grin
could help them believe that life is worth living and
that they should try to get stronger. *Oh, yes. Oh, yes.*

"I want a lot from Christmas and life," Edwina
confessed happily.

"Oh, I do too," Mildred agreed instantly. The ideal
of Christmas had not worn her out. The reality of a
burdened Christmas had taken a toll, however. She
and not just the world had been adding to her own
burdens was a growing revelation inside of her. She
could feel the knowledge of her own complicity of
turning Christmas into burdensome work coming to
light, and she was willing to understand it—and
repent.

"Everybody does," Dixie interjected. She had come
back inside and joined them to listen. The two new
friends had known she was there, but the intensity of
their discussion about a recipe for an ideal fruitcake
had not been stopped to acknowledge her.

"Christmas is why Millie Budge and I ran away from
home this morning. We want a lot and we…." Dixie
began, but didn't finish her declaration. It was the
beginning of something new in her, however. Mildred
saw that as plain as day. Dixie had said the words,

153

"We want a lot...." That was new for Dixie. Mildred grinned and nodded.

"I believe I will make that fruitcake soon. There's no time like the present to celebrate being born again and truly alive," Mrs. Bopp said. "I could start work on it soon and have the first version ready by Christmas Eve. I haven't even started on the spices yet! But I will, and when it is first made, I will give it away to saints and sinners headed home. That's the desire of my heart born right in this minute. Do you hear me, Jesus?"

"Which am I?" Dixie asked suddenly.

"We are all both," Edwina said with a smile that no church lady could characterize with a single adjective. "But once you say yes to Jesus, you are immediately free to stop worrying and live in the moment."

"Yes, we are all some of both," Mildred agreed. "We are all broken together, and we are all getting fixed together."

"I'm broken, and I'm getting fixed?" Dixie asked.

Edwina, Mildred, and Buddy all nodded, smiling, smiling, smiling. *Oh, yes. Oh, yes.*

Edwina continued with her plan, the smile fading to one of conviction and promise born of faith: "Perhaps, if the Lord allows, my newly invented Christmas Stocking Fruitcake will come out for just a little while as the sun is beginning to set...."

154

"And the stars are getting ready to shine...." Dixie added.

Edwina nodded, *yes, oh, yes.* "The fruitcake should be presented to the world as people are headed home where loved ones are waiting and fires are crackling in the fireplace and a candle—any kind of a candle could be glowing in the window. I can see that fruitcake as plain as you," Mrs. Bopp said, slapping the tops of her thighs with both hands and standing.

There was a look on her face that reminded Mildred of pictures of explorers that she had used with fifth graders to introduce the people who had gone out into the world to discover its lands and seas and returned home with news that there were treasures to see, to find, to bring home, to enjoy.

"I'd come back over here for a piece of sublime fruitcake on Christmas Eve if I could catch a ride," Dixie said, and her eyes lit up like a child's. "And we saints and sinners...." She waited for the others to agree that she understood the nature of home life they all shared.

Yes, yes, they nodded. *Oh, yes. Inside the love of the good Shepherd we are all saints and sinners.*

"We could stroll down Main Street together just before the moon comes out and the afternoon has worn on and dusk is falling, and we could look through the storefront windows because two days later the decorations will be out of date. Time flies, doesn't it? For one last walk down Main Street, we could take it all in. This place. This Fountain City where saints and sinners are welcome. Broken people like me," Dixie agreed eagerly.

Wonder filled Dixie's voice as she looked ahead to what felt magical to her. And Mildred could almost see it herself. How the street would look and the lights would glimmer and the late afternoon would be chilly, and because it would be late in the day there would be no issues with parking. People would have gone home early, and then she and Dixie would drive home and the view of the Alabama River and the skyline of Montgomery would be more beautiful than any picturesque card produced by Currier & Ives.

Before Mildred could finish that thought, Mr. Fixit reappeared in his doorway holding a small purple velvet bag. "Look what I found," he said, holding up the pouch. "This is why the angels couldn't fly."

17

A PEARL OF GREAT PRICE IS WORTH GETTING

Dixie, Mildred, Mrs. Bopp and everyone else in the room stopped and looked at Mr. Fixit.

"What's in that bag?" Dixie asked, her face still lit up from the imaginings about Christmas Eve to come.

"Whatever it is doesn't belong to me," he said, looking at Mildred.

Mildred discreetly pointed to Dixie.

Buddy smiled, and brought the purple velvet pouch to Dixie.

"I get to open it?" Dixie asked. "Should I wait until Christmas morning?"

The room was united. Everyone shook their heads, *no. Don't wait. Don't wait. Enjoy the present moment. This moment. This gift. All of us together.*

"Whatever you find will be yours," Mildred promised.

Confronting the mystery inside the purple pouch, Dixie instantly regressed. Gone was the self-assured woman who could hold sharp scissors open and slice through the bad kind of tape. Dixie's fingers fumbled unsuccessfully with the string that had cinched the opening of the pouch. And then blinking rapidly, she laid the pouch on top of the recipes she was taking home. The unexpected undeserved gift immobilized her.

Buddy stood by, his head nodding gently the way a person with a light tremor sometimes does, but his was not a tremor from a muscle or nerve disorder. He was just encouraging her to receive the gift.

Mildred and Edwina played their parts in creating a buffer of sound while Dixie got up her nerve.

"I shall name that fruitcake Christmas Stocking Fruit Cake," Mrs. Bopp repeated more loudly than she needed to speak.

"Will you kindly send me the recipe?" Mildred asked, almost timidly in a voice similar to the one Dixie used when she was feeling younger than she looked.

"If you know the ingredients you have the recipe. You have the whole cake inside of you already. That's a big surprise, isn't it? To wake up one day and discover that you can create all kinds of dishes if you know the ingredients. When you know what those ingredients are, it's just a question of believing and trying, walking in faith—on water, if you like that idea. All you can ever do wrong is fail, and that's quite an adventure in itself. I've created my best recipes from failing many times before I got to the place where I called them sublime."

"I like the idea very much," Mildred said. *You could wear dainty pink slippers while you walked in faith and baked a Christmas Stocking Fruitcake.*

The music box started playing again. The sound started suddenly. While Dixie was considering what to do with the pouch, Mr. Fixit moved the music box closer to Dixie to keep her company. The elegant green tree was secure on top. The key had been turned, and the music was playing. The angels were making their appointed rounds.

"I wonder what that song is. I don't know that song," Mr. Fixit said. "Does anyone know that song?"

"If Frank Sinatra didn't sing it, you don't know it." Mrs. Bopp teased, going to the counter where she helped a customer choose a pie.

"I do," Mildred Budge announced with the same gusto that Mrs. Bopp announced the invention of a Christmas Stocking Fruitcake. "I know the song from just what I've heard—the notes it does play. I know the ingredients of that song, and I believe I can play it."

Mildred Budge turned and moved toward the piano. She lifted the lid and looked at the poor white keys that were all beat up. It was an old piano. A very old piano. Its age was one of the things that drew Mildred to it. She had made friends with many older pianos, finding the response of the keys and the way they fit her hands more comfortably than the digital pianos she had stumbled upon in various stores and fellowship rooms where a different kind of electric piano was supposed to replace an old-fashioned seasoned one that wasn't finished producing music. She liked the wood of the piano. She liked the height of the piano bench, which put her right in front of it where her arms could be positioned at just the right angle to reach the keys. Lowering herself onto the piano bench, Mildred thought, 'I know the ingredients of that song right now.'

"You going to play *that* music box now?" Buddy asked. He stood waiting.

As if she were still talking to Edwina about a fruit cake recipe Mildred repeated, more to herself than to anyone else in the room, "Once you know what the ingredients are, you can figure out the rest. Or you can fail," she said with a shrug that loosened the tension in her shoulders even more.

And then Mildred Budge, who had been playing the piano for most of her life, gave her hands permission to move across the keys. Her mind retreated, and she let her hands move freely. They knew just what to do.

When she finished, Mildred played the song from the music box again. And again. She didn't struggle much. She listened to the music in her head and played it on the piano. It was a different kind of listening—a different kind of playing. It required trust.

Behind her the door opened.

Kissing happened, followed by laughter.

Customers came in and left with pies.

Mrs. Bopp gave Dixie something to eat. And then Edwina came over and patted Mildred on the back between her shoulder blades. "It must be wonderful to be able to play by ear."

"Is that what I'm doing?" Mildred whispered, her hands still moving, her newest smile present on her face.

Then she played the Christmas carols that were on her to-do list to practice. She knew them all by heart. She hadn't realized that she knew them all by heart. But she could play them with her eyes closed or open. The sound of Christmas like the aroma of baking pies filled the small shop: "Oh, Little Town of Bethlehem," "Oh, Come All Ye Faithful," and "Joy to the World."

By the time Mildred turned away from playing the piano Dixie was blotting her lips and saying, "That was tasty. That was a good pie."

Mrs. Bopp did not object to the words tasty or good. Sometimes tasty and good were good enough.

The people in the room had not stopped in their visiting and buying and talking with Mr. Fixit to listen to a plain church lady play the old-timey piano with her back to them all.

Satisfied, Mildred stood up. "A fresh Christmastime will always be inside of me now," she whispered. *It always was. I just needed to believe it and then remember it.*

"It's a pearl ring," Dixie announced, holding up a slender gold band with one girlish pearl set in the center. She had eaten and then, emboldened, Dixie had finally opened the velvet pouch.

"A pearl ring," Edwina repeated for Buddy though he was standing nearby.

"It's been a long time since I wore a ring. My last husband divorced me a while back, and I threw my wedding band in the river a long time ago. A long time...." Dixie's voice trailed off.

Mildred Budge closed the piano lid and patted it with gratitude.

"Dixie?' Mildred asked, turning.

The pouch was open on the table, lying beside the music box and the mischievous angels.

Dixie held up her hand. "See my pearl ring," she said, pleased.

"How lovely. That pearl ring suits you," Mildred approved. She was standing, suddenly eager to get home. "Are you ready to say good-bye?"

"You girls leaving so soon?" Mrs. Bopp asked. *There's no hurry. None at all.*

"What do we owe you for the pies and the repair? We've been here a while," Mildred said.

Edwina and Buddy simultaneously pointed to the Faith Promise jar. "Whatever you want to put in. Thank you for coming to see us. We really appreciate it. We both love people," he said. And then suddenly self-conscious for speaking so much, he announced, "I've got a vacuum cleaner to fix for my new friend Charlie," he said more to himself than anyone else.

And then Mr. Fixit whispered something to Edwina, who nodded.

Mildred fished out some money from her wallet. It was the money she reserved to purchase inventory for her booths at the Emporium and now more mystery boxes at estate sales. And she would. In the future Mildred pledged to herself that she would try to buy a mystery box whenever she could. Such adventures they produced!

163

Mildred put in all she had into the Faith Promise jar.

No one kept watch. No one counted.

Dixie came alongside Mildred and asked, "Should I put in my pearl ring?"

"No, you should not," Mildred replied firmly. "That's your ring. You wear it. Are you keeping the jacket?"

Dixie nodded. "When Buddy put the jacket around me, he said, 'Welcome home,' and I thought that was real sweet. Welcome home. Welcome home. Welcome home. Those words are playing in me like a song. Those are good words."

Edwina brought over a mystery box that contained treats. *Who could guess what sublime inventions were packed in there?*

"My darlin' told me that I better not send you home empty-handed," Edwina said, handing Mildred her second mystery box of the day. Her voice dropped to a whisper, "Your sister might be lonely later without him," she said, tilting her head toward Mr. Fixit. "That's possible. They've kind of bonded. Later when the moon is out and the wonder of the music box has become history and she has even forgotten that she only put on her pearl ring today, when the gift of a perfect pearl feels like old news, and that happens so fast, she may miss Buddy. Miracles become common place so very quickly. But for a little while, we had Christmastime together, didn't we?"

Mildred accepted the mystery box with wonder, her spine growing straighter, her arms stronger, the fingers of her musical hands tingling still with the music that was now hers in a way that it had never been before.

Customers were coming in and going past her to the pie counter, and Edwina Bopp needed to turn and see to them. There were pies to be sampled—pies to be enjoyed and shared.

She didn't hurry. There was no rush. Mrs. Bopp smiled her lit-up smile and said, "Merry Christmas, Mildred Budge."

18

KISS ME GOOD-BYE

I t was hard to leave. Mildred stopped on the threshold and caught her breath before taking the first step out on the sidewalk of Fountain City's Main Street.

Mr. Fixit saw Mildred slow and stop underneath the kissing ball. A gentleman, he walked over and kissed Mildred on the back of the head, on that tender place that often felt bruised.

The kiss made the back of her head feel better. Mildred walked outside and turned to watch Dixie through the store window be kissed by Buddy and kiss him in return. He whispered in her ear while holding her shoulders. The lights on her Christmas necklace began to blink again and the colors of red, green, blue, and yellow were reflected in the glass of Mrs. Bopp's windows.

"Are you ready to go home, Dixie?" Mildred was hit with a wave of fatigue. It surprised her. Until that moment she had been quite energized. But suddenly, she fiercely wanted to be home.

For a moment it looked like Dixie wanted to just stand on Main Street and take in the moment again. There was a hovering quality in her while she inhaled the afternoon light, the air, inhaled the aroma of the pie in the box packed for them by Mrs. Bopp.

"We're eating shepherd's pie for supper. You and me," she declared. "And the music box works. And the song is pretty. And I'm never wearing this elf outfit again. I have about frozen my butt off all day long."

Mildred nodded and led the way down the street.

In the car, Dixie asked, "Do you want to hear the song again?"

Mildred backed out onto Main Street. There was very little traffic. "Suit yourself. You have a sweet humming voice. And when you hummed along with me in the shop while I played that old piano, I could hear you."

"I wasn't humming," Dixie said. "I was eating. Maybe the angels were humming," she said.

"Maybe," Mildred agreed. *Who can know such wonders for sure on earth?*

"You are the only person on the planet that I don't mind riding along in a car with and who will ride along in the car with me. The only one. I'm gonna scrub those cast iron skillets so you can sell them at your booth. That way the day won't be a total loss for you."

"Nothing about this day was a loss of any kind," Mildred replied truthfully. "And thank you for the skillets." She had almost forgotten that she had not found any resalable inventory.

"I like scrubbing. I've always enjoyed it," Dixie confessed. "You don't think less of me for liking to scrub pans?"

"No, I don't think less of you for liking to scrub pans."

"Or because I wanted to throw those Frisbees in the trees?"

"We can try that again tomorrow. Those Frisbees won't have gone anywhere, I imagine."

Dixie nodded, drifting into the kind of contemplative reverie that comes with a drive across the river and back again. Very soon the view of Fountain City was behind them and only Montgomery and home was ahead.

"The riverboat has gone," Dixie reported. "I like the water. I like the movement of water flowing from here to there around bends," Dixie said, almost pressing her face against the car's window. "Where is the music box going to live?" Dixie asked quietly, staring straight ahead.

Mildred knew that expression. She had taught children for twenty-five years. The expression on Dixie's face was the one worn most often when a child was in great need.

"Would you like the music box to live with you?"

Still Dixie stared straight ahead. It was risky telling the truth, and most often people who had suffered the most couldn't tell the hardest truths for the longest time. "It would make being at home alone easier."

"Then the music box will live with you," Mildred said simply. It was an easy gift to make. Mildred had the song from the music box inside of her now and the surprising knowledge that if she knew the ingredients, she could make more music and a fruitcake, and the idea hit her, a couple of very tasty pies.

"I don't know Jesus because I don't know how to read the Bible. I've tried, but I can't make sense of it. Would you teach me to read the Bible?"

"Naturally," the retired school teacher replied.

Mildred Budge had taught a number of children to both read and to experience the Bible, which is how she thought about reading it herself.

"We'll go home. You can open the mystery box that the pie lady gave us. Have a little supper. We'll start tonight if you like. We'll start in Luke with the story of

Christmas. That's excitement, right there," Mildred promised.

Dixie grinned. "That old man had quite a nice smile in him. And there was something about the pie lady that was sublime. Jesus, they were both so nice."

Mildred nodded, confronting the view of her hometown and how its skyline had changed in such a little while. The light was different. The water was different. Her view of going home and what it would be like when she got there was now different.

She wanted to share the shepherd's pie for supper, and soon, when the time was right, she wanted to be alone and put on her mink-trimmed pink satin slippers and see if she could play that song from the music box again on the piano and write the words to "Welcome Home" because that's what the song from the music box should be named. If she could do that, she would teach the song to the Bereans for a New Year's anthem. They could sing a new song together and laugh and hug each other the way church ladies do when they are happy together.

And she wanted to watch a Bing Crosby movie. Mildred wanted. Mildred wanted. It had been a long, long time since Mildred Budge had let herself want. To want was not wrong. You could have some of what you want. There was time for more than she had

171

believed was possible. Christmas was coming and already here at the same time.

"Yes. Yes, let's go home," Mildred agreed. "We'll eat. We'll read a Bible story together. And then we'll get a good night's sleep and see what the morrow brings."

"Tomorrow can't possibly be better than today," Dixie said wistfully.

"But it can," Mildred replied easily. "The days get better and better all year long. That's Christmas for you."

They drove into the early afternoon sun. And inside of Mildred Budge a new idea sprang up: 'It's not as late as I thought. There's plenty of time. Time for everything."

Mildred's Christmas to-do list was growing again, and she knew it. But Mildred Budge was smiling.

Mildred Budge pressed down hard on the gas pedal and zoomed toward home.

Turn the page for a bonus sample of the prequel
to this story: Christmas in Fountain City
■■■■■■■■■■■■■■■■■■■■■■■■■■■■■■■■■■■■■■

BONUS EXCERPT FROM CHRISTMAS IN FOUNTAIN CITY

WELCOME TO FOUNTAIN CITY

"Who died?" Tom Matthews asked, after picking up the phone, which was ringing too early in the morning for it to be any news but bad news.

"Nobody that I know of, Tom," replied a woman with a high-pitched voice who obviously expected Tom to recognize it. He didn't. Caller ID identified the phone call as originating from the Fountain City hospital.

"Then what's up?" he asked, feigning more alertness than he felt while checking his bedside clock. It was 7:04 am. He had slept in. Reluctantly, Tom swung his legs over the side of the bed.

"I just figured you would want to know that some boys used the city's welcome sign last night for target practice. There are red and green paint splotches all over it. Maybe if somebody got over there sooner rather than later, the paint could be scraped or washed off."

And then her voice became a whisper, intimate. "You don't happen to know what kind of fudge Mrs. Bopp is making this year, do you?"

Tom shook his head before he said the word, "No."

Nobody knew the flavor of this year's miracle fudge until Mrs. Bopp showed up with her newest recipe the first Tuesday after Thanksgiving. She spent all of Monday making the candy. People imagined that she had spent the whole year creating that recipe.

"I just figured since you are her landlord, and today is Tuesday...."

"Only for 12 days and she doesn't pay rent. My contribution to Faith Promise is to loan her a vacant store on Main Street to give away the fudge."

As if he hadn't said a word, the caller continued, "And you are also in charge of the newspaper and Mrs. Bopp's fudge recipes are a kind of news now, so you might know what the flavor is going to be this year," she pressed, adding wistfully, "And could finally get a recipe."

"I don't know," he said tiredly as he did to all of the people who asked him the same question and would until 9 am that very morning when the secret would be revealed. "And I don't have access to her recipes from the previous years, and I don't expect I will have this year's recipe either. If I did, I would certainly publish it in the newspaper if she would let me."

"But you don't have it," the voice confirmed with resignation.

"Nope," he said, as the clock ticked off another minute of his life.

The voice became intense. "Why is Edwina holding out on us, Tom?"

The caller knew Edwina Bopp well enough to use her first name.

He forced himself to sound more polite than he felt. "Mrs. Bopp says that none of the recipes are finished yet. For her, every year is a practice run. Only she never makes the same recipe twice, so she thinks that the recipes are never finished."

As if she hadn't heard a word he said, the caller replied irritably, "I think it's flat-out selfish to keep those recipes to herself. If I had the secret to making miracle fudge, I'd share it. Anybody else would. After all, it is Christmas!" she said emphatically and slammed the phone down.

"And Merry Christmas to you, too," Tom replied with his eyes closed, but there was no one on the other end of the phone to hear him.

"Who really cares about fudge this early in the morning?" he moaned, standing up slowly. The hardwood floor was cold; the air in the room distinctly chilled because he kept the heat on low during the night. Very low. He grabbed an old green sweatshirt hanging on the back of a desk chair and wrestled it over his head as the phone rang again. He looked at the clock. 7:10. Christmas was coming earlier and earlier.

Receiver propped awkwardly against his ear, Tom headed to the kitchen and the Keurig without saying 'Hello.' If the woman was calling back to apologize, let her start first.

The person on the line finally spoke up. It wasn't a woman.

"Tom? Are you there? Are you alive?"

This time Tom recognized the voice. It was Henry the preacher.

Tom flipped the Keurig switch and adjusted the cup to make sure it caught every drop of his morning coffee. "No," Tom said, rotating his shoulders up and back. He needed a long shower and hot coffee—a lot of it.

"I just had a call from Shirley who told me that someone has vandalized the city's welcome sign."

"She called me too, Henry," Tom said. *Shirley? Shirley who?*

"Do you think we ought to go take a look at the sign this morning?" Henry asked.

"It's the first day of our Faith Promise campaign, Henry. We've got plenty to do. Let the mayor or someone on the city council worry about that sign," Tom exhaled heavily. "Let whoever Shirley is call *him*."

"That's what I'm afraid of. The mayor might want to change it."

"Do you think that's a bad idea?"

"Not necessarily. But I like to know what the options are before someone starts telling us what to do. We might be able to repair the sign and postpone a discussion that's going to end up costing money until after the first of the year."

The coffee mug finished filling, and Tom took a slurping first sip while mentally rearranging his day. "All right. Let's take a look at it. Eight-thirty?" Tom suggested, checking the time again. He could make 8:30.

"I'll call Julie Blessing to meet us there. This affects her too."

"Julie?" Tom asked. His cup hovered, poised in mid-air.

"Joe's widow would most likely care about a sign that was erected in honor of her husband's neighborly example to our community," Henry said, and his voice was low and considerate. Tom had heard that tone often when Henry consoled grieving family members. Preaching wasn't Henry's strong suit; pastoring his flock was.

"Julie may not remember that the memorial fund money was used for the city's sign."

Emotions had run high when Joe Blessing had been killed by a couple of teenage boys seven years before. A famous friend to others in need, Joe's friends had thought to keep his spirit alive—the spirit of neighborliness that fueled the Faith Promise campaign. They had collected a tidy sum of money after his death and rather than donate it to any of Joe's favorite causes, they had instead used a good portion of the money to erect a sign with a spirit of welcome instead. It had taken two weeks of talking before the council had decided on the size, color, and the wording of the sign: "Welcome to Fountain City Home of the Faith Promise Christmas."

Seven years ago, it had seemed like a good idea. Since then, people had questioned using a church missions' theme for a civic greeting. After a while, people mostly ignored it. Now, with the paint marring the slogan right at the time when visitors would be making their annual drive over to Fountain City to get their taste of Christmas in the miracle fudge and ideally spend some of their money at other stores on

Main Street, there would be renewed discussion about what kind of message should be on the city's sign.

"Call Julie, Henry. I'll see you in a little while."

Only one cup of coffee, a partially toasted bagel slathered with peanut butter, and a fast shower later, Tom drove towards the city limits and the welcome sign, passing first through Main Street where early birders were gathering in front of Ye Old Fudge Shoppe, temporarily named that by the lady whose homemade fudge always launched the first day of the Faith Promise campaign in Fountain City. The annual campaign raised money to feed the hungry and the poor and, specifically, to pay for the deluxe open-to-everyone Christmas lunch at the church to which everyone was invited. Most everyone in town participated in the annual Christmas banquet, but the person whose fudge started it all was Edwina Bopp, former chemistry teacher and now a famous, fudge-making genius.

Good things happened when you ate her fudge. Maybe they didn't happen right at that moment, but later, good things happened.

That's what people said anyway.

MIRACLE ON MAIN STREET

Mrs. Bopp never could get the front door of any Main Street store to open easily. Impatient for Christmas to begin, the gathering of the saints—the Tuesday morning line of people waiting for Mrs. Bopp's Christmas fudge—simultaneously craved her candy and also blamed her for being older and fumbling on the other side of the door. *If she had let herself in earlier that morning, how come she couldn't open the door now?*

"Which way are you trying to turn that knob?" The man at the front of the line yelled through the glass pane of the door.

His wife had sent him after the fudge, believing that every minute he was out from under foot was a golden minute of peace at home as it was meant to be lived.

"Go get us both a miracle," Norma had said, not looking up from her morning coffee. And, he, not understanding why she was impatient—he was offering to go get the fudge!—waited, lingering in the doorway for the sound of the familiar tones of affection that had bid him go to work for thirty-five years and then welcomed him warmly home upon his return in the evening twilight.

That affection in Norma's voice had retired when her husband did from the job where he had been the outstanding salesman of the year for more years than anyone else ever in the history of the music company which had employed seventeen people in its heyday; but by the time George retired, only eight people remained. Norma's husband had been one of them. George had made a good living matchmaking people to new pianos, used pianos, organs, electronic keyboards, and a very small line of guitars and sheet music.

Standing in line like everybody else, the former outstanding matchmaker of music couldn't quite name what the problem was at home, but he was hoping for a miracle that would restore what had once upon a time felt like home to him and didn't any longer.

"She can't work the lock," Norma's husband explained, turning to tell the other early birds who waited for her fudge the way bargain-hunting shoppers just five days earlier had set their alarm clocks the day after Thanksgiving in order to get to the Black Friday specials.

"Give her a minute," he advised, talking more to himself than the others. He was actively trying to stop himself from the natural move of leaning his shoulder against the door and shoving with all of his strength. *He could get that door open!*

"Can you see inside? How many containers of fudge does she have today?"

George peered through the glass, palms cupping his eyes to improve his focus.

"Not too many. Not enough for this whole group of people, that's for sure." *Why didn't some of them have to go to work?* Being retired meant he was supposed to belong to a special group of people with time to stand in line first for Christmas fudge, but he wasn't the only one with that flexibility in his schedule. The other people waiting in line for the free fudge irritated him.

"There's never enough candy on the first day," a voice behind him announced, sounding irritable, too. "Or the second day. Or the third day. You'd think she could make extra fudge for the first day at least because she knows we're all hungry for it. We've been waiting a whole year! She ought to know by now that we want that fudge, and she flat-out ought to make more of it."

"She's only one woman," another voice in the back of the line defended Edwina Bopp softly.

Other voices of people standing in line and bundled up against the early morning chill coughed up opinions and questions. There wasn't enough fudge for everybody in the line, and they were there first and something about the whole situation didn't seem fair. *Why couldn't life be fair at least at Christmas?*

"Edwina ought to get that widow of the man who died—Joe Blessing—to help her. The one that started this whole business. I don't think that lady even participates in Faith Promise. I've never seen Julie Blessing turn in any money to the Faith Promise campaign is all I'm saying."

Voices up and down, back and forth the line, asked:

"How much money do you think we should give for one container of fudge?"

"If you had to buy it, I figure it would be about eight bucks a pound. Ten dollars tops, unless you are buying fudge from someplace like Neiman Marcus, and we aren't buying fudge from there. We're buying fudge from here, Fountain City, Alabama."

"Technically, we're not buying fudge. We are accepting free fudge and giving something in return."

"Oh, mish-mash. I've heard Faith Promise explained a dozen different ways. It's money for missions is what it is, and getting some fudge in order to give some money is just a funnier way to give money is all. And if you get a blessing for giving, well, that don't hurt nuthin', does it?"

"I thought we were supposed to pray about giving an amount we didn't have and couldn't see how we could get and then wait for God to provide it. I thought that's what Faith Promise is."

"It started like that. Then, people got to wanting to move--to do something--so they pledged an amount and then tried to figure out a way to get it. Earn it. Then, they give *that* money."

Conversations zigged and zagged, moving back and forth from one topic to another, with some comments repeated and others echoed.

"A long time ago, I think I paid about ten dollars for some fudge in Gatlinburg. Only eight dollars for Mrs. Bopp's fudge? Really?"

"I've had fudge from Gatlinburg, and it's not as good as Mrs. Bopp's Miracle Fudge."

No one standing in line discussing how much money to give for missions through Mrs. Bopp for her charitably made Christmas fudge ever brought up the word *miracle* as being the real reason they were standing on a hard concrete sidewalk in the chill of an early winter morning with a Christmas to-do list a mile long, but that word *miracle* hung in the air like the hopeful idea of snow coming to a city of the Deep

South. The idea of spontaneous goodness happening was a part of the energy of the Christmas spirit that pervaded Fountain City.

Bright eyes grew brighter.

Non-singers sang.

Women who had been trying to conceive finally did, and the babies were always proper corkers—9 or 10-pound babies that people bragged about: "I got myself a good fat baby this time. I'm gonna call him Fred. Fat babies named Fred are the best!"

The stories of the miracle fudge had become part of the success story of Fountain City and were more exciting to people than the ones about the town's origin, named Fountain City because of the abundance of natural springs that could be found mostly on the boundaries of town now, one out by the city's welcome sign, a couple over by the cemetery, and other unmarked artesian wells out in the rural hilly parts of the county. There was one over by the Waffle House if you knew where to look.

At last! The front door of Ye Old Fudge Shoppe squeaked. Moaned. Groaned. The way the Bible describes creation sounding until the Lord comes again. Only Jesus didn't materialize with his band of angels. It was only Mrs. Bopp. Ducking her head of tidy grey curls at the sight of so many fudge-hungry people and so early in the morning, too, Miss Edwina (a widow, but in the South after a while people call you Miss again) waved a hand in the custom of Southern belles welcoming strangers to her home.

"Good morning!" Mrs. Bopp said, but her voice was so soft it did not carry to the end of the line of forty people or more talking about this and that and their Christmas to-do lists. She pressed her silver-framed glasses up on her nose higher and wondered if she should have combed her hair better. No sooner had she thought the question than a morning breeze came and ruffled it, sending a shiver down her spine. It was a brisk breeze. She tugged at the sash of her red ruffled apron in the back to make sure it was snug and wished she had worn her thicker forest green sweater because her arms quickly goose-bumped inside the thin white one she had chosen to wear because it had snowflakes on it.

"Welcome," she said, and again her voice was almost a whisper.

She stepped back out of the way as a person near the end of the line called out: "We're dying to know. What's the flavor this year, Mrs. Bopp?"

"I made Vanilla Walnut Fudge this year," Mrs. Bopp said firmly—an announcement that was sure to be controversial as people automatically assumed that all fudge was meant to be chocolate. Even white chocolate was chocolate, and she had previously produced a White Chocolate Mint Fudge that had been very well received indeed.

Mrs. Bopp had thought of last year's fudge as her wedding vow renewal fudge, but she didn't call it that. The recipe was inspired one morning while in prayer and asking God's blessings for the marriages of her friends, most of whom seemed tired out by their matrimonial alliances.

"It's only vanilla this year," Norma's husband reported dejectedly to the others in line, and Mrs. Bopp saw something happen that she had always feared would occur if she didn't make some version of a chocolate fudge.

The man's shoulders slumped as if Christmas was ruined.

A steady woman who had lived long enough to manage her reactions to other people's disappointment in her, Mrs. Bopp was prepared for that very human reflex born of habit. She held out a pink beveled platter of generous sample bites and, smiling bravely and encouragingly, Mrs. Bopp offered the disgruntled man a taste of the Vanilla Walnut Fudge, wishing that she had a bite of her White Chocolate Mint Fudge for him because there was something about his impatience that signaled a deeper trouble at home. The creamy sample cube of vanilla candy was sticky to the touch and fragrant with vanilla and something else-- maple. She had almost called it Maple Vanilla Walnut Fudge because she had used both flavorings, but vanilla was dominant. It was best not to confuse people with too many words— even Henry the Preacher believed that!--and besides, she had many notes in her journal about a possible maple fudge that might come into being one day. One day. One future Christmas. If the Lord willed it.

"Do not be hasty in jumping to conclusions, dear man. Vanilla has an allure of its own. It can call forth a quickening of the senses that enlivens hope—a fearless hope. Enjoy today. Taste and see." She did not add that she considered it her springtime-now fudge, invented for people who suffered from that dreadful under-recognized and often undiagnosed depressive condition that comes upon some people in the wintertime: sunshine deprivation. Vanilla Walnut Fudge was a taste of spring in winter. In the eternal spring of Mrs. Bopp's heart, all was always calm; all was always bright.

The restless man took a proffered sample piece of the vanilla candy and placed it quickly in his mouth to *chomp, chomp, chomp*. But he was stopped from that automatic human impulse to consume, to devour and swallow. Instead, the instantaneous anointing of his senses caused by a heavenly creamy sensation and melting vanilla-ish flavors stopped time for George.

Just like that, the forward motion of fearful living stopped, the incessant pull of past times let go its drowning grip, and the gentle hovering embrace of the present moment enveloped him. George was no longer retired. Norma's husband was simply and blissfully vibrantly alive and as young as he always had been. That was his experience of Mrs. Bopp's vanilla fudge.

"S'pretty good," he murmured ruminatively after opening his clear blue, little boy eyes and wondering with a start how long he had gone into what had felt like an inner-body experience. His early morning headache that had come upon him every day since he had retired was gone—just like that. Vanished. He eyed the other sample pieces on the pink beveled platter and wanted to scoop them all off with one swoop of his palm and stuff them in his pockets. It was only that potentially Christmas-ugly crowd behind him that kept him in check. But, boy, was he glad he had come out early. *Was that why they called it miracle fudge? Could it cure you of your daily post-retirement morning headache? What else could it do? He wanted a lot—some for now and some for later.*

Mrs. Bopp had held the plate steady the whole time and was ready to give the forlorn stranger another taste when he said in a voice louder than he intended to speak, coming to his senses, and

192

embarrassed to have lost track of himself: "I guess I'll just take a couple-a boxes. My wife wants me to bring her some."

"Oh, I am so sorry to disappoint you," she murmured. And Mrs. Bopp was disappointed. "But there is only one free box of Christmas fudge per visitor. And please, only free-will donations desired. The Lord loveth a cheerful giver," she promised brightly. Her innocent deep brown eyes shone with a sincere affection for Norma's husband that he did not understand.

His blue eyes grew troubled, surprised that he could not have just what he wanted for Christmas.

"My wife would want to have that recipe if you've got it printed out on a card somewhere. Be happy to throw in an extra dollar for the recipe," he prompted, fishing out a five-dollar bill and a handful of change that would probably come to a dollar. Close enough, anyway.

"Sadly the recipe is not available at present," Mrs. Bopp said with a gentle smile of *I'm sorry.* And she was. Mrs. Bopp often thought about creating a recipe book but the chore of it overwhelmed her, and while she had a tidy record of the exact ingredients for the seven types of fudge that she had invented for her friends in Fountain City, she wasn't sure how to describe exactly the ways to make the candies, which was often about smell as much as taste and pacing too-- learning the enlivened patience of bringing the sugar slowly to a rapid boil. Then, once it had heated oh-so-gently to that soft ball stage, she leaned over it, murmuring, her face bathed in the steam that beauty spas could make a fortune on if they had ever thought of it for facials.

When the fudge had bubbled for her, she had found herself briefly waltzing in the kitchen, happily. The air felt homey and the fragrance almost musical; she couldn't not dance. Mostly while cooking fudge, she kept it company in a motherly way; and when it was ready to be delivered of itself, Mrs. Bopp turned off the burner and readied the nuts and any other flavors to be added, and got ready to stir and stir and stir. The fudge-making wore her out. But she did her part because the Lord loveth a cheerful giver and giving your energy and attention to his good works appointed for you to do was more important than any money you flung into a jar or collection plate. She had learned that being a cheerful giver didn't mean you wore a smile on your face while you labored for others. It meant that you did the work that was your work to do with resolve--sometimes while waltzing, sometimes not--and hoped that there was meaning in it other than the praise that often came, "S'pretty good fudge."

None of this showed on Mrs. Bopp's face as she walked down the line of determined people intent on getting their fair chance at a Christmas miracle, and asked as brightly as her soft voice would let her, "Care for a taste of spring this winter morning?"

No one turned down the free sample, reaching for the small square of vanilla fudge while waiting in turn to grab a single container of the year's delicacy with the other.

It was a simple transaction to make. Yet, people who were usually in a hurry lingered there, staying in the present moment with the woman who had the recipe for something more ineffable than fudge, and so they asked her questions as a camouflage for not wanting to leave after all but were unable to ask exactly what they wanted to know.

A former chemistry teacher, Mrs. Bopp was accustomed to how and why people ask questions, and she was resolved to answer them, though no one asked her the kinds of questions that would have produced confessions of her own personal faith in the energy of life let loose by Christ. Jesus' birth had broken through a time barrier and released a cleansing, revitalizing energy that continued to move across the earth. But no one asked her about that. The questions asked of her were the type that had fill-in-the-blank answers or multiple choice responses.

They wanted recipes. And all she could say clearly and unequivocally was, "Merry Christmas," and then her breath would catch waiting in glad expectation until the other person said what people in Fountain City knew to say which was the truth, "God's peace."

Those four words proclaimed the whole story of Jesus and in so many ways, the whole Bible too, from beginning to end. Eternity was acknowledged. Life-affirming changes were believed, and new fulfilling futures imagined. Hope literally sprang eternal. It was the essence of the Faith Promise commitment, and it had become after Joe Blessing's death the Fountain City way.

For many people about town also had their Faith Promise jars and their Faith Promise activities to meet Faith Promise pledges--just like the old Scrooge who worked at Buddy's Shoe Repair Shop two doors down from the temporary location of Ye Old Fudge Shoppe.

BOOKS BY

DAPHNE SIMPKINS

Belle A Mildred Budge Friendship story

Miss Budge Goes to Fountain City A Mildred Budge Christmas story

The Bride's Room Book 3 in the Mildred Budge series

Lovejoy, a novel about desire

Blessed, stories about caregiving

The Mission of Mildred Budge Vol 2 short stories about Mildred Budge and Friends

Christmas in Fountain City a stand-alone Christmas story about neighbors celebrating together

What Al Left Behind essays about what Alzheimer's leaves behind for the caregiver

A Cookbook for Katie a memoir about love masquerading as a cookbook

Mildred Budge in Embankment Book 2 in the novels

Mildred Budge in Cloverdale Book 1 in the novels

Miss Budge in Love, Book 1 short stories about Mildred Budge and friends

The Long Good Night, a memoir about caring for a parent with Alzheimer's

Nat King Cole: An Unforgettable Life of Music a biography for children 5th grade level

DAPHNE SIMPKINS

Daphne Simpkins is an Alabama writer who celebrates church life with her Mildred Budge books. Connect with her on Amazon, Goodreads, BookBub, Twitter, and Facebook.

Made in the USA
Coppell, TX
08 August 2022

81134137R10115